The

Bellus

Project

Leon Michaels

Books by Leon Michaels

The Path Home

From the Mists of Darkness

Task Force Nemesis

Tales From The Bench

The Hanover Throne

The Echelon Factor

The Morbius Expedition

The Bellus Project

Random Acts Of Science Fiction

"The Crane Equation Trilogy"

The Crane Equation: The Early Years

The Crane Equation: Rebuilding a Nation

The Crane Equation: The Crane Legacy

"The Black Ops Series"

Operation Damocles

Operation Dokkeabi

Operation Yofune-Nushi

Operation Kartikeya

The Black Orchid

The Twenty-First Special Operations Group:

Book One: Family

Book Two: Operators

As Always, I would like to thank my wife for tolerating
My long hours, secluded from her as I write.
Plus, her sharp
Eye in finding mistakes both misspelled words and
Sentences which make no sense what so ever.

My thanks to Mr. Balmer & Mr. Wylie.

And once again to all the ScFi writers from the 40's, 50's,
& 60's
Who paved the way for hack writers such as myself.

A New Mission

Federation Marine Senior Lieutenant Michael James Denoyelles sat at his desk reviewing the previous days training reports of his recruit training company. Eight years in service with five campaigns under his belt along with two wound stripes on his uniform jacket, and he was now the Company Commander of a Recruit Training Company on the planet Denoyelles named for his family.

Michael was twenty-eight standard years old and the Great-Grandson of Duke Conrad Denoyelles, the last Count of the Hanover System. Officially Michael was listed as a Baron, meaning he was in line to assume the royal title of Duke Denoyelles. Conrad Denoyelles had effectively ended the rule of the Three Worlds of the Hanover System by royalty, and the title of Count was buried with him. Currently Michael's Grandfather was the Duke Denoyelles, and Michael was in no hurry for his father to assume the title before him.

He was interrupted in his review of the training reports by his desk communicator requesting his attention.

"Denoyelles here." He answered the incoming call.

"Michael, Cameron here. I need to see you in my office as soon as possible."

Major Cameron Sukowa was Michael's cousin by his father's elder sister.

"No problem Cam, I'll be right there."

As the connection broke, Michael began to wonder why the head of Special Projects for the Federation Marines wanted to see him. If this had been a social call, Cameron would have said so. Michael put the reports aside, pulled on his battle jacket and told his clerk where he was heading in case someone needed him. He took the units ground vehicle since it was eight kilometers from his office to Marine Headquarters.

When Michael arrived at the Special Projects Office, he was directed to a conference room down the hall where he found his cousin and two fleet officers wearing Intelligence branch insignia. His escort closed the door behind him as he entered.

"Lieutenant Denoyelles reporting as requested." Michael announced.

"Michael, thank you for coming." His cousin replied. "This is Lieutenant Commander Parrish and Senior Lieutenant Lancaster of Fleet Intelligence. They have something they wish to discuss with you."

Lieutenant Commander Parrish stood and offered his hand.

"Lieutenant Denoyelles, please take a seat while we brief you on our situation."

Michael shook the Commander's hand, then the offered hand of the Lieutenant before taking a seat at the conference table. The Lieutenant operated the tables Holograph controls and a planet with two moons appeared over the table. The Commander began the briefing.

"Lieutenant Denoyelles, this is Planet N63158. It is located eight parsecs outside the Southern rim of charted space and we became aware of this planet through captured slavers last year. The Fleet would like you to survey this planet to determine the viability of establishing a forward base on it."

Michael looked first at the Holograph, then the Commander.

"Excuse me Sir, but since when does a Marine survey a planet for the Fleet?"

"Since a survey drone reports life on the planet of unknown origin, and according to the slavers interviewed concerning this planet, it is haunted."

"Haunted? Care to explain that further?"

"According to the slavers, when they tried to establish a base of operations on N63158, they suffered several mysterious deaths

2

and destruction or theft of property. They tried to locate the natives of the planet without success. They gave up their base there and moved on to another planet which we have now secured. But there is something else about N63158 which has been kept quiet, even from the rest of the fleet."

The Holograph projection changed to show ruins. But unlike some ruins of single buildings or small communities which had been found on other planets, this first Holograph was of a major city stretching for kilometers in all directions. Michael leaned forward and adjusted the projection with his fingers and even expanded it to get a better look at the view. He had seen this before in a different context.

"Commander, ruins like this have been excavated on Hawking's World, but I think you already knew that."

"You're correct Lieutenant. That is why we have come to you."

Michael leaned back and looked first at his cousin then the Commander.

"Explain yourself Commander."

"It is because of your Grandmother, Ireesha Denoyelles that we have approached you for this mission. The Fleet does not wish a repeat of what happened on Hawking's World after your Grandmother's people were discovered there."

"Then I suggest you isolate the planet, and move on as the slavers did Commander. Or is there something else you are not telling me?"

"Lieutenant Denoyelles, since the ruins on Hawking's has been uncovered, there has been several major scientific discoveries buried in those ruins. If the ruins on N63158 correspond to the ruins on Hawkings, it is hoped that further discoveries can be made and that the answers to a long list of questions can be answered. If the inhabitants of N63158 are of the same classification as the Centaurians of Hawking's World, we must approach any search of the ruins with caution in order not to disrupt their path as we did with the Centaurians."

"Commander, I know of dozens of Centaurians who would be better suited for this mission, why me?"

The look on the face of the Commander was almost one of embarrassment.

"Because you are only one quarter Centaurian, and do not have the adaptive fur of the people."

Michael looked at the Holograph, then stood and walked to the windows of the room, and just stood thinking as he looked out them. He did not turn as he made his next comment.

"Let me guess. You need someone with the racial past to explore what may be another colony of Centaurians or Centaurian like people before a final decision is made on how to deal with the planet. Major Sukowa is also a quarter Centaurian, but he also has Altairian blood in his veins which gives him his light lavender tint to his skin. What makes you think that my genetic condition would be any better than any others for this mission?"

"We don't know if it would or not, but you did your university on Hawkings and your thesis was on the effects of Human Normal Culture on the Centaurians. Then there is the fact your Uncle Abraham recommended you for this mission."

Michael turned sharply back at the table at the name of his uncle.

"How is Abraham involved in this?"

"If you determine it is practical for the Fleet to move onto N63158, he'll be leading a scientific team to examine the ruins."

"Alight then. How many are going on this survey mission?"

"Just you. There will be a Frigate in orbit with an extraction team on standby to remove you from the planet if needed, but otherwise it will only be you with boots on the ground."

"I'll need all of the intelligence gathered up to now including the statements of any slavers questioned. Then I want the logistics estimated for the mission to go over, so I can add or remove items from the list if I feel the need to do so. I'll accept the assignment only once I have the intelligence I feel I need and the equipment I deem is necessary, not what some desk jockey thinks I need."

"I believe that can be arraigned Lieutenant Denoyelles."

"When does the Fleet expect me to begin the survey?"

"As soon as possible. Your uncle is pushing hard to get onto the planet and begin his teams research."

"You can inform my uncle I said he was to take a pill and relax. I'll do the survey by my schedule, not his."

Cameron laughed knowing how Abraham Kerekes would react to being told to relax by his nephew. Abraham being the younger brother to Michael's Grandmother Ireesha would not like his great-nephew giving him orders in such a manner.

The rest of the meeting concerned the outline for the survey and the equipment Michael would take with him plus, how to manage the resupply of rations if needed.

It would take two months for Michael to digest all the intelligence on N63158 and for the Fleet to assemble all the equipment Michael was to take to the surface of the planet.

Since the slavers had landed on the planet in shuttles, a small twelve place shuttle was obtained, then stripped of all unnecessary seats and interior dressings for Michael to use as his landing/support craft. It was loaded to its maximum allowable weight configuration with what Michael determined he would need on the ground.

He boarded the Frigate Rostislav and met his eight-man extraction team. During the two-month flight to N61358, he studied the maps constructed by survey drones for this mission. He also found himself sharing his bed with a female Sub-Lieutenant from the Frigate's Communications Department, who was from Sukowa in the Hanover System.

N61358

The drop went as planned with Michael landing in what appeared to be the city square of what was being called Alpha on his survey map. He was very careful in landing to place his shuttle on a level spot and not hit any trees or the remains of statues within the square.

For an hour Michael let his sensor pack sweep the area around him to determine if his landing had garnered the attention of any inhabitants of the planet. The only reading her received were for small, minor animal life that had already been deemed non-dangerous by the slavers that had landed and cataloged that life form.

Michael had landed just at day break and according to the data on the planet, he would have approximately fifteen standard hours of daylight before darkness fell on the area. When he left the shuttle, he was outfitted with a two-liter water bladder inside his small reconnaissance pack along with two days of compressed rations and a lightweight shelter if needed.

In his vest, he carried a variety of items for first aid and comfort along with an emergency transponder that he could either activate to alert the evacuation team to know to extract him, or it would automatically activate if his bio-rhythms hit a dangerous level as if he was injured.

His weapons included a large knife strapped to his right leg which could be used as a machete to clear brush or to fight with if necessary. There was a standard One CM pistol hanging and strapped to his right thigh if needed along with a needle stunner pistol in a holster on his vest. A smaller field knife was also attached to his vest for a variety of purposes such as skinning animals for food. On his left hip was a special purpose hatchet/pick combination tool with a saw inside the handle which would cut through light metals and wood.

Strapped across his back was a one of a kind sword, a katana forged on Hawking's World by a master blade maker which if given

6

enough force, would slice neatly through plastron body armor. This was a gift to him upon graduating the university on Hawking's World by a relative of his grandmother. He had spent countless hours learning to use such a sword and the rituals that went with it as he progressed through the university. It was made known to Michael that because of his desire to learn about his distant heritage, and to protect that heritage, he was the only 'furless one' to possess a sword of this type. Normally only pure-bred Centaurians owned one of these swords.

The Hawking's Institute on Hawking's World had given him a list of things to look for during his survey. He had a plasticized map with grids placed upon it which he would search each grid completely before moving to the next. Michael did a quick, but thorough search of the grid the shuttle was sitting before moving out to the next grid.

The AI in Michael's helmet was linked to the sensor pack in the shuttle and kept him advised of any possible danger lurking in the shadows of the ruins. He could feel he was being watched, but the sensor pack never alerted him to the presence of another life form as he walked the grids moving, shifting debris as he looked for signs like the ones found on Hawking's World.

When he found something that he felt might interest the archeologists from the Hawking's Institute, he had his AI note the location which was then relayed to the shuttle, then up to the Frigate for later reference. Besides looking for artifacts or other things of interest, he was looking for signs of human, or even alien activity.

No trace of the aliens who had taken humans from Earth to Hawking's World eons ago had ever been found, other than the ruins they left behind. Was this planet another location for kidnapped humans as Hawking's World had been?

Michael searched the grids until three hours before dark to give himself enough daylight to return to the shuttle for the night. He sealed himself inside the shuttle and just laid on his bunk as the sensors watched for intruders.

Foot Prints

Michael suddenly woke to the feeling he was not alone. He listened for any sound that might alert him to an intruder that had somehow evaded not only the sensor pack, but the shuttle security system. He slowly rolled out of his bunk and looked towards the cockpit at the chronometer to check the time. It was 0413 and he felt the need to void his bladder.

As soon as his feet had hit the floor of the shuttle, soft, red lighting filled the craft providing him with the light he needed to move around the vehicle. In the small sanitizer, he looked in the mirror after he voided his bladder and decided to leave the beard growing on his face. Being a quarter Centaurian meant his beard and hair grew faster than human norm, even if he was not covered in fur as a full Centaurian would be.

His father had a rich, brown fur covering his body and his younger sister was covered in a rare, ginger red fur. Because of her red fur, his sister was highly courted, especially since she had reached maturity which pleased her, but gave their father fits at times. Michael would often quietly chuckle at the fact his sister swore no man would have her until her wedding bed, but she was playing the males who courted her for everything she could get without taunting them with her favors.

Michael went back into the shuttle and noticed his weapons laid out on the small table where he had placed them the night before. All his bladed weapons were removed from their sheaths except for his katana which was partially pulled from its sheath about ten centimeters. Everything was neatly arranged as if someone had laid them out for inspection. The problem was, he had not unsheathed a single blade when he had laid them on the table. Someone had been in the shuttle and yet, the security system had not alerted him to the intrusion.

This anomaly had been covered in the statements from the captured slavers as they said things moved during the night to include some equipment dismantled with parts scattered across the ground.

Michael did not believe in ghosts, especially ones that were neat in their actions. He had a suspicion concerning the ghost stories in the reports, but needed more information before he could formulate a theory. But inanimate objects do not move on their own without being acted on by an outside force.

He checked his gear to insure nothing else was messed with, then fixed his breakfast since it was near his normal time to be up. Michael checked the shuttle's logs for any anomalies just in case something registered, but did not set off any alarms. He came up empty with his search of the logs and just sat back in his command chair, opened the armored shutters to the view screens and watched the sun come up.

Michael knew there were ways to fool or get around sensors, but this shuttle was fitted with the best, most sensitive sensors the Federation had available. That told Michael if someone out there was in fact canceling out the sensors, they were far advanced in technology than the Federation.

As he exited the shuttle for the days exploration of the ruins he paused and looked at the ground near the shuttle. Nothing appeared to be disturbed more than it had been from the landing and there were no foot prints or animal tracks near the shuttle hatch that were not his own. He closed and sealed the hatch then remotely set the security system on it before moving to the next grid on his map to explore.

The grids he was following took him into building ruins when he felt they were safe enough to explore by himself. Before he had left on this mission he had visited with his Grandmother Ireesha concerning her younger brother Abraham. His grandmother warned him that Abraham would sacrifice him to the mission of gaining scientific knowledge in advance of others especially if it answered questions concerning how the Centaurian Tribe came into existence.

Michael spent seven days moving through the debris littering the grids. Two grids were covered with what appeared to be the remains of a large building which had collapsed from eons of neglect. Artifacts found exposed were photographed and left in place for any team which would probably be forth coming once he completed his survey.

Every morning he found items within the shuttle to have been moved as he slept. If he neatly lined up his things on the table, the next morning they were in disarray, but if he just tossed them onto the table, they might be neatly arranged the next morning. There was no DNA evidence or fingerprints of any nature on his gear except for his own to point him in a direction of causality.

During the day, he could almost feel eyes on him as he moved through the debris of the ruined city. Michael picked up a small, ceramic statuette from the debris of an animal he was not familiar with and took it back to the shuttle. The next morning it was gone. He went back to the location he had found the statuette to find it had been returned to that location from where it was discovered.

Michael took the statuette back to the shuttle, rigged a simple booby-trap under its base, and went back to exploring the next grid. When he returned at the end of the day, he found traces of the white powder that was released that the booby-trap expelled when it was disturbed. Inside the shuttle, he saw the shuttle floor covered in the powder, but what excited him was footprints in the powder.

The footprints were small, almost childlike is size, telling him that the individual that had been caught in his trap was small in stature. This could be that it was in fact a child, a female, or a race of human-like creatures that were inherently small, such as the Polyexnian's who, because of the heavier than Earth gravity, developed into a stunted growth with the average individual barely standing one meter tall.

Polyexnian's were extremely strong, stronger than the normal human and highly intelligent. They filled most of the Combat Engineer's within both the Free Lance Infantry and the Federation Marines. The formation of the prints told him they were wearing some form of smooth bottomed covering, shoes which did not allow for the display of toes or such in the powder.

He went back outside the shuttle and looked at the surrounding ground closer and found a single print in the soft earth. Once more it was a small print, and the pattern of it in the soil began to look familiar to him. It reminded him of the animal skin moccasins worn by Centaurians in the deep forests of Hawking's World.

Michael sealed the shuttle and activated the automatic cleaning program and waited until the exterior control panel indicated it had finished its cycle removing the powder residue from the interior surfaces. After his evening meal, he filed his nightly report leaving out the part of having an uninvited visitor. At no time during his daily reports had he reported the visitations to the shuttle, or the feelings of being watched as he moved about the city.

One thing that concerned Michael was if he reported the visitations, Abraham would immediately bring a team onto the planet to find the residents in his desire find the answers to his questions concerning the Centaurians. Grandmother Ireesha could not explain why Abraham was so obsessed with discovering more information concerning the creation of the Centaurian race.

He felt he had at least another week left in exploring the ruins before he might consider shifting to another group of ruins to search them. His mission was scheduled for a month total before a decision was would be made for him to either leave the planet or continue with the exploration of the planet.

Michael's own curiosity about his nocturnal visitor was something he knew he had to control until he had the city covered. One thing he felt secure in concerning his visitor, if it was a single individual, was that he was not in fear of his safety. Even the slavers had commented no one was injured even during some of the strange mishaps they had experienced when they first landed.

To Michael, the visitations were designed to cause him to leave the planet. He could not deny a small level of fear that he would become a victim of these visitations if he stayed, but he could not leave his own questions concerning the planet unanswered.

If these ruins were from the same people who kidnapped Earthlings in a failed attempt to prolong their own race, how is it no evidence of space travel has been located on Hawking's World, and the orbital survey of this planet does not indicate a single space port where a suborbital craft could land.

Now he had a situation where orbital survey's and the constant scanning by the frigate overhead for life forms had turned up nothing, yet Michael knew he was not alone. Or could it be that what has been discounted as animal life was human in form?

That evening he checked his sensor log for any animal life form that came within five meters of the shuttle. Nothing was reported larger than what might be considered a rodent about the size of a domesticated feline, or house cat. Unless the individual who had set off his little trap was a shape shifter, they had somehow defeated the sensor pack.

Michael filed his evening report once more leaving out the intruder incident.

The Council's Decision

As Michael was filing his report, a meeting was occurring a thousand kilometers from his location. Within the meeting chambers sat twelve inhabitants of the planet Michael was surveying with a single individual standing before them. The individual before the council was a female, standing approximately one point five meters tall, weighting fifty-six kilos at her last physical two months before.

The Council leader questioned her.

"Kaya, we understand the human you have been watching set a trap for you today. Are you in good health?"

"Jiazi, it was a harmless powder like was once used to tend to infants. But it did cover me, and caused me to leave trace of myself within the vehicle itself."

"That is good to hear that you were not harmed Kaya. Now, we have the results of the Genetic Profile Tests on the human. I believe you will be pleased to know he has markers which fit the Master's Profile. This is the first human we have encountered to have those markers. None of the last humans to come to Bellus had any of those markers."

"That is good Jiazi. Hopefully he is the one our race needs."

"Kaya, are you still intent on giving yourself to this off-worlder?" One of the male council members spoke.

"Titus, I know you would rather have me on your bed, but you agreed to this program from its inception. But keep hope Titus in that he may not wish to have me and may want another. I will say this for you Titus, you are more attractive than our guest."

Although there were several choked laughs from the council no one spoke for several moments.

"Kaya, what are your plans now?" She was asked.

"Saoirse, since he is a viable candidate, I now must make my presences known to him. Time is running short for our people. If this experiment is not successful, we are lost."

"Kaya, I am concerned about your own future. Our people still have several generations at our current rate of decline." Titus spoke up.

"Thank you, Titus, but our people are more important than myself. Unless the Council instructs me not to follow the path of the plan, I do not feel I have any other choice in the matter. My father predicted our downfall and projected the path we must take to survive. I shall continue his work and walk this path as it is set before me."

"I've known you for too long Kaya to think I can prevent you from following through with this experiment." Titus responded. "As much as it may pain me, I wish you success in this matter because success for you means success for our people."

"Thank you, Titus. If the Council will excuse me, I must make plans for allowing this individual to discover me."

"One last thing Kaya." Jiazi spoke up. "Have you discovered this human's name?"

"Yes Jiazi, he is called Michael Denoyelles and he is a warrior, not a scientist. I've been able to lightly touch his mind as he sleeps, but it is a risk. Each time I have touched his mind, he awakens as if he can sense my intrusion into his dreams. This could be a result of having the Master's Genetic traits within his cells, except he is unaware of the talents buried deep inside of him. I think it would be a matter of caution not to make him aware of what lies beneath the surface of his mind."

"The Council agrees with your warning Kaya. We shall insure all of the people are aware of your warning if you are successful in bringing him into the fold." Jiazi replied.

"If the council has no other need of me, I shall take my leave and prepare for the next step."

Kaya left pondering if Titus or the others felt her lie. She thought Michael was a beautiful specimen of man and was developing a desire to have him.

A Glimpse of Beauty

For several days Michael lost the feeling of being watched or having the shuttle invaded. He also noticed that during this time he slept undisturbed through the night. At first, he missed the feelings of another nearby as he also wondered what the source of feelings were telling him. Michael was beginning to feel alone for the first time since arriving on the planet.

It was mid-day and he had four grids left to explore before consideration of moving to another location and searching there, when he felt once more that he was being watched.

From the first moment he had stepped upon this world, Michael had always maintained his face shield down to enhance his vision. But as he considered how the intruder had bypassed the sensor pack, and the security system of the shuttle, maybe it also blanked out his vision using the face shield. Michael raised his face shield.

As he moved through the grid he was working, he only lowered the face shield when he needed to record a specific item for the exploration team to consider at a later date. Twice during the exploration of the grid, he caught just a glimpse of movement out of the corner of his eye. He had seen animals at different times, but this was no animal.

Once he completed the grid, Michael exited towards the area he had seen movement and found foot prints like the one outside the shuttle. Michael smiled to himself thinking that whoever it was out there watching him had decided to up the game and let themselves be discovered. He looked at the direction of movement and compared it to the map he was using. His watcher was guiding him out of the city into the forest, but only if he took the bait.

Michael stood and looked around the area not so much as trying to locate his shadow, but to allow that individual to see him as he turned back towards his shuttle. He took his time returning to the shuttle as he fought the temptation to look at his back trail to see if he was being followed.

16

As he walked back to the shuttle, he could feel the pull of returning to the footprint and following it. He paused, cleared his mind and focused on removing the pull from his mind. It felt as if a string snapped as he felt the pull release from his mind.

Michael considered what had just happened, and his ability to exercise control over his mind. He had read of the possibility of individuals with physic abilities, but no hard evidence had ever been discovered on the subject. If the individual or individuals that were watching him had such abilities, how is it that he could remove or block their intrusion into his mind?

Once again, he filed his report leaving out any mention of the glimpse of what he considered a human like creature that was watching him, and he was not going to mention the possibility of physic abilities of that creature. But if the natives of this planet had physic abilities, then that would also explain the deaths of several of the slavers in preventable accidents.

He did not have the feelings of being watched the rest of the evening as he ate his evening meal, then later took his shower before lying down. Just as sleep took him he felt a wave of calm flow through his mind and body. It was as if someone was telling him he was not at risk.

Fifty meters from the shuttle, Kaya sat crossed legged on the ground as she meditated, reaching out to Michael's mind to give him a feeling of peace. She only brushed his mind since he had built a wall she could not penetrate without him realizing what he had done. Kaya knew she had to develop a new path for him to follow in discovering her. Granted, it would be simpler for her to just expose herself to him, but this was a game she felt he would appreciate more than the forward approach.

For the next two days, Michael would only catch a fleeting glimpse of his stalker, but never one which might give him an identification of sex or species. He cleared the last two grids, filed his last report on those grids before determining his next move. Before he lay down for the night, he received a message from the frigate that a ship from the Hawking's Institute would be in orbit within thirty standard days with the exploration team, meaning his Uncle Abraham would soon be on the surface.

When he woke in the morning he found an interesting message laid out on his table. The blades he carried along with his eating utensils were formed in the shape of a heart. The meaning of the message eluded him, but it caused him to set aside any movement away from this city until he examined the possibility that he could contact his stalker. It was almost as if his stalker was telling him to come and make contact, yet the meaning of the heart eluded him.

Michael left the shuttle and stood thinking which way he was to travel. In grid five, there was a large pool of water which seemed to come into mind, and he smiled thinking whomever it was out there was trying to tell him which way to go. He checked his map, then headed for the pool.

Kaya smiled as she felt him accept her hint to come to the pool. She prepared herself if not for the actual meeting between them, but for him to finally see her.

Even before Michael reached the pool, he could see someone, or something in the water at the far edge of the pool. He never tried to hide his movements as he moved towards the pool, and finally stopped at the edge looking at the subject in the pool. It was almost one hundred meters between him and the individual in the pool, and he could not tell the sex of what appeared to be a human, but one thing stood out was the wet, silver hair glistening in the morning sun.

Michael stood and watched as the individual moved from the pool to the edge and stretched. They then turned towards him and there was no doubt the individual was female. From this distance, he could tell this female was as in good a physical shape as any female Lancer or Marine, including the female Centaurians that he was familiar with. Her pubis was the same color as the hair on her head, and she made no attempt to hide herself from him as they stood looking at each other.

She reached down and picked up an article of clothing, then began to pull it over her head. It was a simple earthen brown smock which came down to mid-thigh. She next picked up a belt with a long knife on it along with several pouches and wrapped it around her waist. He watched as she slipped her feet in slippers, then bent over one last time to pick up a sheathed sword and hung it over her back.

Kaya looked across the pool at Michael, smiled, then walked into the underbrush and disappeared. She picked up the shielding device she had lying on a downed tree and continued to move away from the area.

Michael smiled to himself and knew what had to be done next. She was leaving it up to him as far as meeting, and he was going to do it on his terms. He laid out his plans in his mind as he walked back to the shuttle.

The Meeting

Michael set up his field table under a tree next to the shuttle and set two chairs at it. He had gathered several fruits from the surrounding area that had already been tested and were safe to eat, along with being very flavorful.

He did not have fine china or crystal goblets available, only metal plates and cups suitable for hard field usage. As he was doing this he opened his mind and placed a picture of him and her sitting at the table, sipping a fruit juice from cups with fruit upon the plates. He wasn't trying to contact her, but if she could get into his head, he was going to let her see this scene he was setting up.

As he sat at the table with his back to the shuttle, he wondered if she would come and meet with him. Michael had no idea what the protocol was for such a first meeting, but he felt he had made it innocent enough that if she was desiring a meeting, then the stage was set.

Patience was a virtue of any Marine since all too often, they had to wait for events to take shape before any action could be taken from administrative matters, to actual combat. Michael sat at the table with only his katana at hand for only a short period of time before he saw her exit the thick underbrush approximately two hundred meters away.

Michael stood and watched as it almost appeared she was gliding across the distance between them. Her movements were graceful, almost sexual with each step she took on the debris littered terrain. Her long, silver hair would sway to her steps and often catch a bit of the breeze and flutter around her, unnoticed by her as it seemed she was focused on him. The only feelings he could distinguish was one of desire, but what that desire was could not be defined.

Kaya felt like she was about to explode. Her stomach was quivering from the anticipation of meeting this man, and even with all the planning she had made for such a meeting, she was at a loss on what to do once they were face to face. She had no idea how this human judged beauty and desire since she had never been able to delve that deep into his mind. Would he accept her when it came time to further her father's plan? He was much taller, larger in frame than the men of her race. Could she accept him if the final steps were taken without great pain? Would he even consider joining with her to hopefully produce an off-spring which could revitalize her race? Kaya suddenly felt afraid of this man she was approaching.

Michael watched as she came closer and could feel apprehension on her part. He tried to project a sense of calm, security in that he meant her no harm, but was unsure if she could sense that projection. As she came closer he was able to obtain a much better view of this female.

When she stopped about a meter from the table, Michael indicated her chair and tried to put on a smile which he hoped would ease any apprehension she was having. He could tell she was nervous and had to laugh to himself that she had been in the shuttle at night with him, but now they were in the open, both awake and within reach of each other.

Kaya watched as he indicated for her to sit and the smile she saw on his face was genuine. It dawned on her that since the first time she had seen him, asleep in his craft, his hair had grown long, almost to his shoulders and his facial hair had covered his face. But his dark eyes seemed to sparkle as he smiled at her, telling her that he meant her no harm. Kaya smiled and took her seat as he moved to his and sat down.

When Kaya sat she realized her sword was uncomfortable in its position, so she slowly removed it from her body and laid it down beside her chair. He was also wearing his sword and she had noticed that was the only weapon he had visible, unlike when he was searching the ruins. He saw what she was doing and copied her action by removing his sword and placing it on the ground next to him. In this they were now equal, except she felt he could snap the strongest man of her race in two with his bare hands.

Michael looked at this vision of beauty sitting across from him and decided that he had never laid eyes on such beauty in his life. Her hair looked like polished silver framing a heart shaped face. Her lips were just full enough to accent her face with a perfectly shaped nose. But it was the eyes that drew his attention. They were almond shaped with silver eyebrows, and the color of her eyes was almost startling as they were a bright, emerald green. He had never seen eyes of this color before, and they seemed to beckon him to join with her.

Kaya examined him as they sat, looking at one another. She remembered his face before the growth of his bread and his strong jaw. Then her mind remembered how she viewed him lying on his bed with only a coverlet over his manhood. His large chest with dark hair covering it and the scars of battle upon his body. He had a body of pure muscle from what she suspected were hours of harsh work. No man within her race was formed in such a manner.

Michael finally broke the silence as he picked up a large plate covered with fruit and offered it to her.

"Would you care for something?" He asked her.

Kaya looked at him realizing she could not understand his speech. She knew she had been able to understand his mental language, but his verbal speech was foreign to her. Kaya accepted the plate then sat it down and looked at him as she spoke.

"We do not speak the same language. This needs to be rectified."

Michael could not understand what she was saying, but her voice was almost musical in tone and texture. But how were they to bridge the language barrier?

Kaya could tell he was confused as she was, but had only one option left at this juncture in their meeting. She reached out, laid her hand on the table palm up, and waited to see what he would do.

Michael looked at her hand and saw her long fingers waiting for his reaction. He knew she wanted him to take her hand, but in what manner? He placed his hand next to her with his palm up and let her make the move he suspected she wanted. Kaya looked at his large hand and smiled as she moved her hand to his and just laid it on his, palm to palm. The effect was almost immediate.

It felt as if an electric current was flowing through their hands, back and forth between them. Unlike the natural reaction of being shocked where an individual would jerk their hand away from that which is shocking them, this seemed to cause them to weld them hands together.

Michael closed his eyes and it was as if flares were popping behind his eyelids as his mind opened, and it became a computer hard drive being updated with a new operating system. Kaya shivered as she felt volumes of information flowing into her mind. She had only meant for this connection to give them the means of communication, but it seemed it was working in both directions with a visual play of words from his language.

What seemed to go on forever only took microseconds before Kaya's hand seemed to be ejected from atop his. She shook in her chair, unable to open her eyes as a sudden pain seem to strike her in her forehead, then vanished in that same second. When she opened her eyes, Michael still had his closed, and his body was quivering from the exchange.

When Michael opened his eyes, he could see that she was shaking from the experience.

"Are you alright?" He asked her.

He was speaking in his native language and Kaya knew exactly what he was saying. She replied in her language.

"Yes, I am fine, thank you for asking. I was not expecting such a transfer of knowledge."

Michael heard her speak in her language and understood her speech and meaning. They could now communicate.

"Then please relax, as I mean you no harm. My name is Michael, and I would like to know more about you, and your people."

"Michael, my name is Kaya. What is your purpose on being here on Bellus?"

"We call this world N61358 as we have not given it a name. But Bellus is as fine a name as any. My purpose is to survey, looking for specific evidence of an ancient race which once visited my mother planet, Earth."

"Yes, we know of Earth. My people came from there also. I suspect the ancient ones you refer to are the ones we call "The Masters". Our knowledge of them must be greater than your own."

"Yes, that must be so. The only knowledge we have of that race was that they took Earthlings in order to search for a way to save their own race. There is another group, or race of humans which has been discovered that we call Centaurians, that suffered the same fate as yours. Except your fate seems to be gentler than theirs."

"How so Michael. We have knowledge of another world which The Masters had taken Earthlings too, but not where it is located, or the results of their research. We Bellusarians are also the results of a failed experiment to extend their fate."

Michael knew she was asking for knowledge of the Centaurians and felt it would be proper to extend that knowledge in hopes she would return with knowledge of her own people. He gave her everything he knew from his studies on Hawking's World. He held nothing back concerning the Centaurians as he described them in detail. When he finished, he realized she had been nibbling on the fruit as he spoke, and the shadows of nearby trees had fallen over the table. He leaned back, took a long drink from his cup and just looked at her.

She put down the piece of fruit she was nibbling on and took a drink of fruit juice before speaking.

"Michael, you are well versed in the history of the Centaurians. How is this so?"

"Because my Grandmother Ireesha is a Centaurian, and I was educated on Hawking's World. One moment and I will show you."

Michael left the table and entered the shuttle. When he returned he sat a small holograph projector on the table and activated it. The first image to appear above it was his Denoyelles grandparents. The next image was of his Centaurian grandparents, then his own parents. Last was the image of his sister in the costume of a Centaurian female warrior, black knee-high boots, dressed in the black leather thong and halter with her sword in one hand and her half mask in the other.

"Michael, this explains much about you."

"How is that Kaya?"

"We have your genetic profile from a sample I was able to take while you were asleep. Like my people, you carry genetic material which is from The Masters. It was a concern of my people if your race could mate with ours because of the Masters genetic material in the genes."

"Why is there such a concern Kaya?"

"Michael, I cannot explain now. But I do have one important question of you concerning the Centaurians."

"Ask your question Kaya. I will answer the best I can."

"By now you are aware I can enter your mind and see what you are thinking. This is a trait given to my people by the Masters, and the use of it is highly restricted since it also can be a dangerous weapon. My reaching into your mind was to learn from you only that which was your intent for this world, but I was never able to reach that deep without awakening you. You have the same ability to reach into my mind, even if you are not aware of it. This is why we can now speak to one another. Is this trait common amongst the Centaurians?"

"No Kaya, it is not, and it is a talent none of my race are aware of as far as I know. Look into my mind and see I am speaking the truth."

"I do not have to look anywhere Michael. Your emotions are strong with fear of that ability unknown to you. Why do you harbor such fears?"

"First answer me this. Why is it a concern that your race can mate with mine?"

"Michael, I cannot answer that right now."

Michael stood and looked down at her.

"Then until you can answer that question, we are done here. I've kept your presences a secret to the people I report to, and will continue to do so, but until you answer my question, we shall have no further contact. Good day Kaya."

Michael picked up his sword from the ground and walked to the shuttle.

"Michael!"

"What Kaya?"

"I am not free to give you that answer now."

"Maybe, but I am free to ignore you until then. Goodbye Kaya."

Kaya reached out with her mind to try to encourage him to stay, but found a wall erected to prevent her subtle touch. She made no attempt to penetrate any deeper into his mind. From even before she sat down, she felt his desire towards her, yet he closed those feelings behind a door and walked away from her.

Michael entered the shuttle and secured the hatch behind him, then leaned back against it while wiping the sweat from his brow. He felt her pull to return to the table, and her as he fought it with every step he took. It was a relief when she released the pull to return and he relaxed. Kaya was a highly desirable woman and he had to fight the desire to be with her.

He went to the command console of the shuttle and checked the sensor pack to see if it had registered her attendance outside the shuttle. Once more it only showed him outside. Michael had touched her, she was real as real could be, and yet, the sensors failed to register her. Whatever technology was available to her was superior to what he had available.

Then he had a frightening thought. What if he did have latent psychic abilities from what she called The Masters? If he had the ability as a quarter-blood Centaurian, what of the full-blooded members of the species such as his Uncle Abraham? It was not known within the universe at whole, but Abraham was a bigot.

Abraham blamed the 'furless' ones for ruining the lives of the Centaurians even though because of them, he was able to be educated in the manner he had been. He tolerated Grandmother Ireesha's family because she was the matriarch of their clan, but it was well known within the family of his dislike for 'furless ones'.

If Kaya had plans which included him, he certainly had to make plans to use her to prevent people like Abraham from gaining a source of power which could not be protected against with the weapons at hand. A psychic could cause an army to turn their weapons on each other, and allies into enemies.

How he could use Kaya in this manner was unknown to him, but he knew if the universe was to maintain its status quo, he would have to find that key to keep this secret locked away.

Kaya walked back to her small transport vehicle knowing she had failed in this first attempt to bring Michael into the plan. She had also told him more than she should have during their meeting. Now she had to either make the decision on her own and face the consequences alone, or take this to the council and possibly face the ridicule of Titus and others. If they ordered her to remove herself from the project, she knew she would find herself eventually mating with a man she could never love.

No, she thought to herself, she was not in love with Michael, but the thought of finding herself mated to Titus felt like death itself. She would not return to the council and report what happened, but would sleep on the problem and face the possibilities tomorrow. Kaya folded out her vehicle command chair into a bed and removed her clothing to lay down for the night. She looked at the command console before closing her eyes to insure all was in the green, then looked to see if the message board had anything for her. No messages which was a blessing after the mess she had made of the meeting. She fell into an uncomfortable sleep thinking about the future of her race and her own place in it.

Surrender

Michael lay on his bunk thinking about what he had learned during the meeting with Kaya. What was not talked about was why Kaya's people had discouraged the slavers from staying on the planet, and even arranged the deaths of several of them to create the illusion that the planet was haunted. But now they are known to him which placed his own life in danger as he was certain they would not allow him to leave without conditions. Conditions he was not sure he could abide by.

As he fell asleep, he waited for her touch in his mind as he had felt over the days he had been on the planet. It never came to him as he tried to open his own mind to accept her touch. This was a new experience for him as he relaxed as his mind, became open to the world about him.

He awoke with a start as something brushed across his mind as he slept causing him to awaken. Unlike Kaya's touch on his mind, this touch did not feel benign, and he tried to find the source in his mind. Was it a nightmare from his past, or a nightmare which would cause him harm if he allowed it?

This brought another thought to his mind. Where were Kaya's people hiding? Was the touch on his mind from another since he had spurned her? But he had not spurned her, he only put conditions on their meeting. He focused the thought he meant no ill will for the people of Bellus, only peace.

Michael had no idea if he truly had the abilities Kaya spoke of, but he was willing to play this game if it would lead him to the answers he felt he needed before Abraham arrived in orbit. He had seen his own DNA markers which tied him to the Centaurians and except for the genetic anomaly which produced the fur on a Centaurian, his was complete as any full-blood.

Kaya shivered on her bed as she felt his mind touch hers, but refrained from responding to his touch so he would not know how powerful his untrained touch was. She came full awake when the message board alerted her to a message.

29

The message was from the Council and it advised her that there had been an unknown disturbance within the psychic flow of the planet. It asked her if she knew if it had come from her subject since he had the genetic profile of the Masters. She responded that she had no idea where it came from, but had also felt it. Kaya knew it had been Michael, but could not risk the Council taking violent action against him until there was no other choice.

Kaya focused on Michael and sent him a warning that what he was doing was risking his own life. She felt the touch of his mind as she placed the message there, then gently removed herself from his thoughts.

Michael felt Kaya's mind link to his and understood the message she placed there. He was untrained and had exceeded what was governed by the people of Bellus. He was at risk, and needed to be aware she could not help him, if he continued on this path. He slowly fell back to sleep with the understanding he was dealing with forces he neither understood nor was trained in.

When Michael awoke passed his normal time, he wondered if it was because Kaya had done something to make him rest longer than normal, or if it was his own body telling him he needed the rest. He took his time getting ready for the day since he did not have much to do unless he decided to look at one of the unmarked areas on the map.

For the next three days Michael searched the unmarked areas for the signs he was given without any success. He could sense Kaya was near, but she made neither physical or mental contact with him during this time.

Kaya just watched Michael move through the debris of the city and pondered the possible results of his knowing the truth behind her mission. Do his people bond upon mating, or do they just enjoy the emotion of mating, then move on until they do bond with another. If her father was correct, all she needed was his offspring's genetic material to develop a serum which would end the decline in their own genetic profiles and allow the Bellusarian race to continue.

She remembered her father looking at the strain on her people's genetic profile telling her that even a normal human would help strengthen their own. The problem with her race was the small population left behind when the Masters disappeared, and over the eons, the genetic diversity slowly vanished which resulted in fewer and fewer offspring each generation.

Kaya knew she needed Michael if she was to finish her father's work, but was unsure if he would be willing to provide what her people needed. But she could also feel apprehension in Michael, but was unsure of the cause of that feeling. Time was running out for her in that the Council was asking her the status of the project.

She concluded that she had no choice in the matter but to give into his request. Kaya went to his craft to find the table and chairs still set up, but cleared of any manner to eat. She smiled, then went to gather fruit for the table.

Michael returned to the shuttle and as he cleared the thick underbrush he saw Kaya sitting at the table with what appeared to pieces of fruit laid out on it. He smiled knowing she would give him the information he required, but even with that smile was the question of what price he would have to pay for that information. As he approached the table, Kaya stood and removed her sword then laid it on the ground behind her chair.

"Is this a social visit or one of exchange?" He asked her as he drew close.

"It can be both Michael, if we can find common ground."

"I have yet to see any creature, animal requiring a sword for defense. Are you capable of using that sword against a threat, or is it because I carry mine?"

"Interesting question Michael. Elsewhere on this planet are creatures which without a weapon would find a person a delightful meal. They are not in this region during this season, but they have been known to travel through here as they migrate in search for food. You mentioned how the Centaurians were masters with a sword which I suspect was taught to them by the Masters who

31

taught my people, so they could protect themselves before we were left to fend for ourselves. Yes, Michael I have been trained to use my sword and it was forged specifically for me. Why do you carry yours since you are also armed with weapons more suited to your being?"

"I carry it because even my other weapons have been known to fail. And there have been times where a projectile weapon was not practical."

"Michael, I sense sadness in that statement, but please do not allow that to take away from our meeting today."

"Kaya, have you decided to answer my question, or shall I just leave you out here alone with the fruits of your labors?" He motioned towards the fruit on the table.

"Michael, I will answer any question you feel you need an answer too."

"Then allow me to put my things away, and get something to place the fruit on as we eat and talk."

He went into the shuttle and placed his weapons on his table, then collected the plates and cups needed for their meal. She met him at the shuttle hatch and took the items from him, then told him to clean himself for the meal as she prepared it. He returned to clean up from the days travels thinking she sounded like his mother when he came in from playing for the evening meals.

When Michael exited the shuttle, he stopped and watched as Kaya cut up the fruit into small bites and placed them equally on the two plates. She was using a long, thin bladed knife that he did not remember seeing a sheath on her belt for. He watched her hands move with speed and grace as the razor-sharp blade dissected the fruit in swift motions. Yes, he thought, she knew how to use a blade.

Kaya looked up to see him watching her as her hands continued to move over the fruit, cutting it into chunks for eating. She never lost her sense of where the blade was as it sliced through the meat of the fruit close to her fingers holding it. She finished the last cuts, placed the portions on the plates, then poured a small amount of water from her canteen on the blade before wiping it off with the hem of her smock. She reached down, picked up her sword and slid the blade into the pommel of the sword until a distinct click could be heard as it locked into place.

"Come Michael. Eat and talk with me." She spoke as she laid the sword back down.

"Kaya, you talk, I'll listen."

She nodded her head as she took her chair and watched him as he took his. He picked up a piece of fruit and just popped it into his mouth as he looked at her. Kaya took a deep breath before speaking.

"Michael, my race is dying. Our genetic diversity is lost, and each generation produces fewer children to sustain our people. It is estimated we have six generations left before we become as those who stole our ancestors from Earth. We need an infusion of new genetic material to stay viable."

"So that's what you meant when you said I was suitable for mating?"

"Yes."

"Kaya, setting aside your mental abilities and the color of your eyes and hair, you are still human as are the Centaurians. You can mate with any human and keep your race alive."

"That is true Michael, but the genetic markers which you carry from your Centaurian ancestor makes you even more valuable since we also carry those same markers. Your genetic material in a child from a Bellusarian mother would not dilute the genetic pool as would a normal human."

"Kaya, in about thirty days, you will have actual Centaurians walking on the surface of Bellus."

"Explain that please."

"Kaya, I am surveying the planet for scientist from the Hawking's Institute. They are coming here to search for some tie to those who you call the Masters. I do not know what they are actually looking for, but they are coming."

"Michael, this is not good. If they have latent mental abilities such as you have, then they are not only a danger to this world, but to the universe. We are trained from an early age how and when to use this ability to prevent harm. If a single individual arriving here awakens that talent and is dark of heart, then the damage they can do is too great to imagine."

"Answer me this Kaya. I have the best sensors available to our fleet on my shuttle, and yet it does not register your presences here. How is this?"

"When the Masters left, they left us with technology far greater than your own. It is with that we have remained hidden from you and others. But even it has its limits. Those that recently came before you stumbled upon us and suffered death to keep that secret."

"We have time to work on keeping your secret Kaya, because I know of at least one individual coming here that would take advantage of the powers you possess. I am a warrior who is sworn to peace. I only take up arms to insure others, the weak can live in peace and prosper."

"Michael, I felt that about you the first time I entered your mind. It is why we are sitting here talking instead of my staying hidden from you."

"Setting the problem of the others coming here aside, what about me? What are your designs for me now that I am aware of your problems?"

"I wish that you would give me a child to help strengthen our genetic line."

"Kaya, what good would a single child do to help your race survive?"

"When that child is old enough, we can make a serum from its blood. That serum would strengthen our genetic profile, and my race would be able to once again become viable."

"Sacrifice a child for the sake of your race?"

"Oh no Michael, we would only take what is safe from the child. I would never harm a child, especially one that came from my own body."

"Well that is good to know. But what of your people? Are they willing to insure the safety of a child, even if means the death of their race?"

The question caught her off guard as she suddenly realized that there could be individuals who would think nothing of taking a life for the sake of the race. Before she could answer he spoke again.

"Then there is another problem Kaya. Any child I produce could have the traits of a Centaurian such as being covered in fur as is my sister. How would your people deal with that?"

"I do not know Michael. I'm afraid some would think them a freak of nature, and refuse to accept them into our world."

"Kaya this has happened before in my world. My Grandfather's Father fought against such bigotry. We have races with different colored skin. Different being far from what would be found on Earth. But Earth normal was the common acceptance until my ancestor broke those bonds and insured everyone, each human regardless of outward traits was accepted as an equal. There are still problems on some worlds, but time will erase those. But your race will introduce a new set of traits which I am afraid the universe will not deal with kindly."

"This is something we have not considered. After those others came, it was discussed that their humanity was almost non-existent. They gave off a brutal aura which made removing them easier than we thought it would."

"Kaya, those people were slavers. They take humans by force from their worlds and transport them to others to do the labors others will not do, or want a high reward for doing. They also use them for their own purpose in labor, or as sex slaves, often both. I have fought three battles against those people, and I have seen things I do not wish to see again, or wish to talk about."

Kaya leaned back in her chair and looked at Michael for a long time. She did not try to reach into his mind because she could feel disgust and hatred for those he called slavers. It dawned on her that the link they shared when they merged so they could speak to one another was still intact, even if it was a very thin link.

Before she could speak he continued.

"Kaya, events are unfolding that no one could predict. Slavers came here and discovered the ruins, then were captured by our Fleet. They gave this information about Bellus to our people, who gave it to the Hawkings Institute since it is of an archeological nature. Now the very people you need to refresh your race are coming, but with them comes the danger of destruction. Destruction on a scale I cannot even imagine. I will do what I can to prevent this as it is a responsibility of my family, my clan to fight against such destruction even if it means my own life."

"You would fight against your own people to protect those you do not know?"

"It is the fate of my clan. And knowing about your mental abilities makes in even more important that secret is protected. I cannot allow such power to fall into the wrong hands."

"Thank you, Michael. It is for the Bellus Council to make the final determination concerning those coming to Bellus. I will have to inform them as soon as possible, and ask that you stand before them to give your evaluation of the situation."

"If they require that of me, I will go before them and tell them the truth as I see it. Now what about us? Do you still wish for a child by me, and if so, how is this to be accomplished?"

"Michael, my body is unknown to man. If it is agreeable to you I wish to accept you as a woman, not as an experiment in a lab."

"Kaya, in my world, women give themselves to men for three reasons. Love, enjoyment or profit. Even though I feel an attraction between us, there is no love between us. Since you have never been with a man, then you will not be joining with me for enjoyment. The only profit you will gain from our coupling would be the enrichment of your species, but you must consider that a single coupling may not produce a child."

"I am aware of that possibility Michael. I am also aware that it will be uncomfortable at first. Michael, I have given myself to this project in order to save my race. I do not expect you to bond with me as my mate if you accept me in your bed."

"Kaya, I have known several women during my life, but I have never taken one to bed with less time together than you and I have so far. A DNA test or as you refer to it, a genetic profile, does not give any hint of how a person really is, and those traits can be transferred to others during such an exchange. My children may inherit certain aspects that are not only foreign to your species, but even offensive. Just because my DNA is acceptable for your project that does not mean it will be suitable for your race."

"That has been a consideration Michael especially after dealing with those you call slavers. So, what do you suggest?"

"Do you travel back to your hidden city each night, or do you have a place to sleep nearby?"

"I sleep in my transport vehicle which is near. Why?"

"Move it closer to this location. The closer the better. We will spend the days together as I continue my search, and we will learn about each other. In time, we shall either part with the understanding that I am not suitable, or we shall mate, and hopefully give your race the genetic material they need to continue."

Kaya thought for a long moment before replying.

"Alright Michael, I shall do that. Now eat. You have had a long day and need nourishment."

Michael laughed thinking all women are mothers at heart. Kaya looked at him as if he had gone mad as he laughed then picked up a bit of fruit and ate it.

They talked for over an hour with each exchanging stories from their childhood. Michael could tell she was hedging some of her stories, but figured that was to protect her own people as he kept his as open as he could remember.

Kaya left the table to retrieve her transport and returned less than an hour later. Her vehicle looked to Michael as if it was a covered single seat cargo skimmer such as they used in moving supplies in the field. He asked her if the sensors could detect it and she told him no. Kaya also informed him he could only see it because of the setting she had placed into it. The ship in orbit would not be able to detect it either, as it would reflect the image of the ground it is sitting on.

Michael told her this was another reason to be careful of intruders, even those that come to help. Sooner or later this technology will get out into the universe and be used for evil, making the job of men like himself even more difficult.

They sat and talked well past darkness at the table by the light of the two moons. When he suggested they retire to their separate beds, she stood and came around to his side of the table and kneeled before him, presenting her sword to him.

"Michael, I am yours to take as you desire. My sword to you is my bond that I surrender myself, my body to you at your demand."

"Stand Kaya and retain your sword. Is this part of Bellusarian mating ritual?"

"Yes, Michael it is."

"Interesting. The Centaurians have a similar ritual. This must come from the Masters you speak of."

"Yes, it is written as being so."

"Kaya understand me now. When, and if, I decide to take you to my bed, I will offer you my hand and you will go to it as my equal."

"Thank you, Michael. May you have a good rest this night."

"And to you also Kaya."

Michael lay on his bunk and remembered the words of his ancestor, the Count Denoyelles in his telling of how the Countess came to his bed. He was going to exercise the same restraint in taking Kaya. She was the most beautiful woman he had even seen, and she was willing to give herself to him, but not for the same reason the Countess gave herself to the Count.

There was no doubt in his mind that even though they barely knew each other, there was an attraction between them, but they were a long way from love for each other.

Kaya lay thinking she had followed ritual and he had not shunned her, but had placed his own qualifications to the ritual. He was an off-worlder who was raised with a different set of rituals, but would those rituals serve her people? She had been courted twice once she had become of age, and now Titus wished her, but there could never be love between her and Titus. Titus wished her because of who she is, not because he was in love with her.

No, Michael was not in love with her nor was she with him, but Kaya felt Michael was capable of loving her in time, and she, him. All that matter right now was doing what was necessary to help her people.

Michael was awakened in the middle of the night as he was reaching for his katana. He rarely remembered his dreams or nightmares, but this one was so vivid that it was as if it happened while awake.

He watched Kaya walking towards him bare of all clothing as he saw he at the pool. As she took each step closer to him she changed. Her body slowly transformed as her hips widened to three times their girth, while her firm breasts elongated and hung down. She became stooped in her posture and leaned to her left as her skin became wrinkled and marked with ulcerating sores. Her long fingers became crooked and clawed with blood on them.

Kaya's face became distorted with her eyes changing color to a blood red while her mouth became crooked with long fangs almost down to her chin also dripping blood. It was as she was reaching out to him that he awoke.

He stood, unsheathed his katana, then stepped to the hatch. Michael took a deep breath then opened the hatch and stepped out into the night air. Nothing moved outside as he stepped to the ground in his bare feet. He was holding the katana up along the back of his right arm where he could sweep with it if threatened.

Michael moved to Kaya's vehicle and saw her hatch was also open and she was standing outside with her scimitar shaped sword in her hand. In the faint moonlight, he could tell she was nude as she was looking off into the distance. It was then he realized he was also nude.

"Michael, are you alright?" She asked without looking at him.

"Yes Kaya, I am. What is happening?"

"Someone does not want us to mate. I just had the most horrid dream of you ripping me apart as we mated. I could almost feel the pain of it as I awoke."

Michael told her of his dream, but that he woke before she touched him in the dream. She turned to look at him then smiled as he told his tale.

"Well from what I can see in the moonlight it will be uncomfortable the first time we mate, but not to the point you will rip me apart as in my nightmare."

"Kaya, who would want your project to fail?"

"Michael, I do not believe this was intended for the project to fail, but to keep us apart. Only one person I can think of would want that, because they want me on their bed. But I find no trace of that person in my mind. Michael, what just happened is forbidden by Bellusarian Law."

"Kaya, I will not allow such nightmares prevent us from what may happen. I do know that was not your touch in my mind, but I will not move from my position concerning our relationship, and certainly not to prevent any further nightmares."

"I understand Michael. I'm going to get dressed and go to the capital, so I can speak with the Council in the morning about this illegal intrusion into our minds. Regardless of their decision, I will return as quickly as possible."

"Kaya, keep this in mind and inform the Council of my words. I accept that I am untrained in this new talent my ancestors have given me, and I shall not try to use this talent with anyone except you, within my own restrictions. But if there are any more intrusions into my mind, I will learn how to seal my mind from intrusion, then hunt down the person or persons attempting to scare me aware from you. And when I find them, they can taste the edge of my blade on their neck."

"Michael, they will not take those words kindly."

"Kaya, remind them I am part Centaurian. Those that are coming as full-blood Centaurians. I will do whatever I can to protect your species which means your secrets, but I will not be intruded upon. I am a Denoyelles of the Hanover System and our word is our bond. If the saints decide that I am to mate with you, to bond with you, then it shall be, and anyone trying to prevent that faces me with cold steel. Transmit that to the Council and allow them to feel the anger I know you can now feel from me."

"Michael, they will take that as a threat to their well-being!"

"Kaya, someone is threatening my well-being with that mind game tonight. I have enough of my own nightmares without someone adding to them. Do as I ask, or do not return."

41

"Yes, Michael."

Michael returned to his bunk and just lay looking at the ceiling thinking he had allowed his anger to speak for him. But he also felt that this unseen Council needed to be aware of his anger in what had happened tonight. A normal man would have already taken a woman as beautiful as Kaya is to bed the moment she had explained her mission. But he wanted more from this relationship if possible.

Kaya flew north to the capital unsure of what would happen once she transmitted his comments to the Council. She could feel his desire for her, but his concern for her people and their secret was even stronger. He was hiding something from her which was driving his concern, and if she had read him correctly, his oath to protect them and the secret of their psychic abilities was as honest a statement she had ever heard from any person in her life.

As Kaya entered the Capital Zone, she notified the controllers she was returning to see the Council on urgent business. This would set things into motion as the controllers would contact the Council members advising them of her return, and her need to speak with them. She set the crafts controls on automatic for landing and tried to focus on relaxing before the meeting. Michael's words scared her in ways she never suspected.

Michael rose out of bed and could feel the tension Kaya was feeling as she sat outside the Council chambers waiting for the Council to convene. The link between them was still intact over the distance of separation, and he sent her the feeling of calm coupled with the strength of his convictions.

Kaya felt him gently touch her mind and the apprehension she had been feeling drifted away. She kept her thoughts to herself, but smiled at his touch and sent that back to him. Michael felt the warmth of her smile and closed his mind as he prepared for the day.

Unwelcomed Visitors

Kaya once again stood before the Council and explained why she was there, and why this meeting was so important. The Council had her connect to the Transference Modem, so they could see the nightmare which had been planted into her mind while she slept. They then saw Michael and heard him describe his nightmare.

Since she was still connected to the Modem, she let her mind play the messages he gave her for the Council in his own voice. Once his message was complete, including her protests about transmitting his message, the connection with the Modem was disconnected. Kaya stood shivering from the effect of seeing her nightmare again, and the fear she first felt at his message to the Council.

"Kaya, we shall investigate this violation of your, and Michael Denoyelles privacy. This is unforgiveable and will not be tolerated." Jiazi, the head of the Council spoke.

"Thank you, Jiazi. Michael and I are still building trust between us and this could have destroyed everything."

She went on to explain the basis of his oath to protect the people of Bellus and their secret.

"I am aware that the Council has already felt Michael's power as he is untrained, but his mind is open now because of the transference between us so we could communicate. This was unforeseen by myself, and I assume the Council. He is not a diplomat but a warrior, and speaks plainly his intentions. But he is hiding secrets that we must know about concerning the people, the Centaurians that will soon come to our world."

"Kaya, are you still intent in mating with this off-worlder?"

"Titus, I'll mate with Michael, or I'll mate with no man. No, I am not in love with him, but whomever is trying to separate us made a critical mistake concerning both of us. First, they angered him which was not wise. Second, I feel they were doing so to have me. This angered me which is also not wise. Am I clear enough on this Titus?"

"Very clear, Kaya. But may I say he was very bold in issuing a sword challenge."

"Titus, I know you hold a Master's rating with the sword, but you have not seen his. It is of a steel we know nothing about and the little tests I could do on it says it is stronger than anything we possess. He is a warrior who carries the scars of battle. The people who made his sword and taught him to use it were also victims of the Masters, so I would not call his challenge so much as being bold, but made from confidence in his ability to use that sword."

"Kaya, then I stand properly chastised."

"Kaya, your defense of this Michael almost sounds like a woman in love defending her mate." Svenja, another Council member spoke.

"Svenja, I do desire Michael, but I agree with him that we do not know enough about each other to declare we are in love. He is a strong man in body and spirit. I would probably agree I am enthralled with him considering he is unlike any man I have ever met in my short life."

"Are you sure your emotions are not clouding your thinking as far as your project is concerned?" Council Member Marcus questioned.

"Marcus, we need this infusion of genetic material. Everyone within the scientific community agrees on this. I hope there is no doubt on the Council that I was willing to give myself to an off-worlder, any off-worlder, that could provide that material. If there is any doubt concerning my dedication to the project now, please be specific in stating so. If I can provide what we need and find fulfillment on a personal level at the same time, I shall not turn my back on the opportunity. But my first concern is the project."

"Kaya, there was a proposition made to just take genetic material from a qualified subject and develop it in the labs for use to infuse into our people." Marcus spoke again.

"Yes Marcus, I remember that it was determined that there was only a thirty-one percent chance of being effective in mixing with our genetic material where a child would be almost one hundred percent successful. Granted, this was before we realized that we might have a donor who has the Masters genetic material in his genetic pattern. This might make the lab results stronger, but it will certainly make a child stronger in many ways."

"Kaya, what are your plans now?" Jiazi inquired.

"My plans are to continue with the path laid before me. The first step in achieving my goal in continuing my father's work is in sight."

"And if you fall in love with this off-worlder?" Jiazi further inquired.

"Then I can only hope he will bond with me as my mate as I work on the project. I have told him the purpose of my contacting him, and he is receptive of his part in it. Beyond that I cannot speak for him anymore than you have heard from his own lips."

Jiazi pushed a button on the table in front of her and a panel appeared in front of Kaya blocking her from the Council as they discussed the situation. Kaya stood patiently awaiting their decision concerning what she had brought them this morning. She shielded her own thoughts as she knew that regardless of their decision, she was returning to Michael.

Kaya lost track of time as the Council discussed the situation she had presented to them. When the panel disappeared, it shook her out of her thoughts. Jiazi spoke for the Council.

"Kaya, first, please let your Michael Denoyelles know that the Council regrets the actions of whomever intruded upon his privacy with that vulgar dream. The Council accepts his words not as a threat to our people, but a promise to protect his own well-being as is his right. Next accept the Councils confidence that you will succeed in your project to protect our race. It is the Council's desire that you learn more about the Centaurians, and their reason for traveling to Bellus. If Michael Denoyelles would come to brief the

Council in person before the Centaurians arrive, it would be greatly appreciated."

Jiazi paused, then looked up and down the Council table before returning her focus to Kaya.

"On a personal note, I hope that you find what you are searching for in your life. You have dedicated years to this project, and have forsaken much for a woman of your age. Take your leave of the Council, and may the Ancient Ones watch over you."

"Thank you Jiazi, and I thank the Council. I will do what I can, and learn what I can from Michael. But I will not do anything which might hinder the project."

"The Council understands your feelings towards the project. Once again, we wish you success."

Once Kaya left the Council chambers Jiazi once more spoke to the Council.

"We have a quandary concerning the intrusion into Kaya and Michael Denoyelles dreams in that if we pursue it as we should, it will embarrass the Council. Titus, I will warn you only once to never interfere with Kaya's project again, or I will call for a tribunal and subject you to the chamber to determine the truth."

"Jiazi, are you accusing me of invading their dreams?"

"Titus, it is well known your desire to have Kaya for yourself. Name me one person who has such a desire for her and I will apologize, but Kaya's own words convict you as all of us know she would never direct such statements at a person unless she was sure they were guilty. She was diplomatic in her wording, but pointed just the same. Titus, you are pardoned from this one mistake in the violation of their minds, but I will set a tribunal if another is reported."

No one spoke as Jiazi stood and left the chambers followed by the others. Titus sat knowing he could not survive a tribunal and that Kaya's words had indeed convicted him of a very serious crime within their society. He had no other choice but to accept Kaya's decision and move on to another to mate with. There was one young female in the Archives that had made slight overtures to the fact she might be receptive of a relationship.

Kaya returned to the camp to find Michael was off exploring another area for whatever he was supposed to be searching for. She knew from the short trips into his shuttle at night that he was a meat eater as she was, and imagined he had only served fruit during their meetings as a neutral meal, not knowing the dietary considerations of the Bellusarian people. It was still early in the day and if he kept his normal schedule, he would not return until late in the afternoon.

She took a crossbow from her vehicle and went in search of fresh meat for the evening meal. Kaya killed a small porcine creature whose meat was pink in color and very flavorful when properly prepared. She hung it from a tree close to the camp, gutted and skinned it then left it hanging to allow all the blood to drain from it as she then gathered certain pieces of dead wood to use as a cook fire.

From her vehicle, she took the survival cooking equipment which included a long, thin metal rod and a pair of forked rods which she drove into the ground for the rod to lay on. Rocks to contain a fire on a cleared off partial of ground were laid in a circle. Kaya ran the rod through the carcass, then laid it on the forks before she set fire to the small pieces of wood already in the circle.

Kaya seasoned the meat by rubbing spices into the exposed flesh, then once satisfied it was ready, ignited the small pieces of wood to act as a base for the cooking fire. As the fire grew, she added wood until she felt there was all that needed to cook the meat.

As the meat was cooking, she went back into the woods and found root vegetables to go with the meat. Back at the camp she prepared the vegetables for cooking in a small pot as she watched the fire, keeping it at a level she felt was necessary to cook the meat.

She left the vegetables in the pot soaking in water after she added a slight measure of salt. All she had to do at this point was to wait for Michael to return before she placed the vegetables at the edge of the fire to cook them, and prepare a sweet, tangy drink from the leaves of a small tree which her people called tea.

Michael returned as she estimated to find Kaya had the table laid out with plasticine cups and plates from her vehicle, and the smell of the meat cooking on the fire. She just smiled at him as he passed her to enter the shuttle to put his things away and get cleaned up.

When he returned, he was clean with a clean shirt on and sat at the table as she moved around between the table and the fire preparing the evening meal. Kaya cut off large chunks of meat off the carcass placing them on a plate to serve from. Once she felt the vegetables were ready, she poured off the water and put them on another plate before she poured the hot tea into cups to drink from.

Michael complimented her on the hot meal as they first talked about the Council meeting, then about his day of exploring the ruins. Once they were done with the meal Michael showed her where to place the left-over food, so it would not spoil so they could eat it another day. Then the conversation turned back to the Council meeting.

"Michael, I have no doubt that a man called Titus was the cause of our nightmares. He has wanted me for his bed since I became of age. I told him he would never have me regardless of what happens between you and I."

"Kaya, under normal circumstances, I would be hard pressed not to take you to my bed the first time we met, but with the consideration of why this is happening, I think we need to be sure this is what we want."

"Michael, I am not trying to bond with you. Even in our society, a single female can enjoy men without bonding, if they are discreet and do not encroach upon another female's bonded mate. As you said a female can bed a man for the enjoyment of the moment. But since I have no knowledge of a man in that capacity, my only desire at this moment is the fulfillment of my father's work. That requires me to accept a man and bring a new life into this world."

"Kaya, what you describe is a very clinical, sterile if you will, approach to what you want from me."

He drained his cool tea and stood up.

"I'm sorry Kaya, I want you, but I'll not take you in such a fashion. We'll stay as we are until you can come to me wanting me for me, not because of your project that is so important to you. No, I do not expect you to bond with me either, but I will not be just a subject of your project, a specimen to use to further that project. Good evening Kaya, and this was a very pleasant evening meal."

Kaya watched him retire to his craft then went about cleaning up the last of evening meal remaining on the table. She thought she understood what he was telling her, but did not know how she was to take that step. Her life until the passing of her father was one of privilege and study. Since then she had opened her life to the world, but had refrained from the sexual adventures many of her peers ventured into.

She carried a Master's rating with the sword and had taken several animals with in as she trained to survive in a dying world. Kaya could construct shelters in the frigid northern regions or the humid, wet regions along the planet's equator. There was nothing she could not do, but she was at a loss where the male of the species was concerned. Nothing in her studies had prepared her for what Michael was presenting her with.

The next two days told her a lot about the relationship they had as he treated her with respect and as a partner in his exploring, but he rarely touched her unless it was needed to cross a piece of broken terrain or ruins. They rarely spoke as it seemed they had already answered all the questions one had for the other. He finally asked her a question she was not expecting.

"Kaya, how old are you?"

"Michael, I am currently twenty-two based on our calendar."

Michael's helmet AI converted the planet's annual calendar to Earth Standard and gave him her age compared to his own. Kaya was nineteen by Earth standard.

49

"Interesting Kaya as you look much younger. I am twenty-seven by Earth Standard dating."

"How old would I be if I was on Earth Michael?"

"I estimate you would be nineteen by the adjustment in planetary orbits."

"I've been of legal age since I was sixteen and an orphan since I was thirteen by our calendar. Am I too young for you Michael?"

"No Kaya, you are not. By your calendar, I am about thirty-five. Is that too old for you?"

"No Michael, you are not too old."

Nothing more was said until he told her it was time to return to the camp. Michael had given her full access to the shuttle since the refrigeration unit was there to store the meats and vegetables she was collecting for meals, instead of eating ration packs. He never saw what she was eating except, during the mid-day meal when she took odd looking cubes from a pouch on her belt as he ate a Marine field ration.

Six days after her return from the Council, Michael did something he had been wanting to do since he first saw her as she walked into his camp. After they had cleared the table from the evening meal, had sat and talked over a cup of her tea, Michael stood, moved around the table and lifted her out of her chair and kissed her.

During their talks, she said she had kissed a boy before, but now she was kissing a man with years of experience kissing some very exotic females. But once they became firmly into the kiss something happened neither expected. They linked again, and she knew what he wanted as she returned his kiss and gave him what he desired. He could feel her own desires as the kiss progressed until he broke the kiss and released her. He stepped back and looked at her.

"Kaya, is that normal with your people to mentally link in such a fashion?"

"I don't know Michael, but if I am not too forward, I enjoyed that very much."

"I enjoyed it too Kaya. But that was a good night kiss, not a kiss in prelude to taking you to my bed."

"I understand Michael, but please do not hesitate to kiss me again if you wish."

Over the next two weeks they kissed each other good night with her coming to him and sitting on his lap one night for a long session before her moved her off his lap. He remembered that she never wore underpants beneath her smock and he was fighting his own desire to take her to bed.

They had shifted campsites a week before and were exploring another smaller city when a call came from the frigate in orbit.

"Survey one this is Rostislav, do you copy, over?"

"Affirmative Rostislav, I copy you clear. Over.?

"Survey one, we have received an emergency beacon signal from a freighter on the rim of charted space and must respond. Do you want the extraction team on the ground before we break orbit? Over."

"Negative Rostislav, all is well here. Good luck on the call, Over."

"Roger Survey one, we'll get back as quickly as possible. Take care down there. We are boosting out of orbit now. Rostislav Out."

Except for filing his daily reports, Michael had ignored the Rostislav in orbit above him. Even as Kaya was stalking him, he never felt he was in danger. Michael watched Kaya as she hunted for fresh meat using her crossbow or rigging a snare. She was always quick on the kill, so the animal would not suffer, and it seemed she was apologetic as she did the deed. Whoever had trained her was on par with the deep woods Centaurians that he had lived with during breaks at the university.

Three days after the Rostislav had boosted out of orbit Kaya was in the middle of rigging a snare when she suddenly stood up, pulled what Michael had always thought of as a bead from the chest of her smock and placed it in her ear. All Michael could hear was her side of the conversation.

"Control, this is Kaya. Do you have something for me?"

"Yes Control, I understand. Thanks for the advisement and please keep me informed as this develops."

She affixed the bead back to her smock as she looked at Michael.

"Michael, we have an unknown space craft entering our system, and it does not fit the configuration of your frigate, or that of the crafts the slavers used when they were here."

"Do your people know where this craft is coming from?"

"They said it was coming from a direction other than what you call known space."

"It can't be slavers after what happened to the group that was here, so it is either free booters, scavengers who are looking for treasure, or raiders who will take whatever they can steal including women. We had best get back to camp and get ready for them. Can you hide my shuttle with your device?"

"No Michael. The vehicle has its own unit and it just covers itself. I have a personal unit which could hide the two of us if we are very close together, but your craft is exposed."

"No problem. Let's go, we have things to do."

When they returned to camp, Michael removed a large net system from the side cargo compartment and with Kaya's help set it up over the shuttle. He explained that it would help break up any sensor readings, and only the most powerful sensors in the Fleet could penetrate it, and standard sensors could only make out a much smaller signature from space.

Kaya was notified when the unknown vessel entered orbit around Bellus and they waited under the netting as it made sensor sweeps of the surface. Michael's sensor pack reported the strength of the sensors on its receptors to be of standard intensity.

When it was reported to Kaya that a craft had dropped from the orbiting vessel towards surface, they waited until the Bellus controllers reported approximate location for landing. It was heading for the large city Michael had already searched and left weeks before.

She received one report that the people on the ground was heavily armed which caused her to move to her own vehicle, and from its cargo compartment, remove a projectile weapon and began loading its magazines with cartridges. Michael asked her why she had never produced this weapon before to which Kaya explained, that it was only for survival if she had to land in the heavily forested region near the equator.

Michael broke out his own rifle, his issue One-CM assault rifle and checked it before insuring his magazines were full and ready to go, before just sitting back once more to wait and see what their visitors were going to do. He had preconstructed a message for the Fleet concerning the visitors, but had not sent it in case they might detect the signal burst, and pin point their location. All they could do now was just sit and wait.

One thing that surprised Michael was that Kaya put on a pair of pants that matched her smock along with thigh-high soft soled boots that had daggers stuck into the outside of each boot. When Michael asked her why she never wore the pants before, she only smiled and told him to figure it out for himself. He could only laugh at himself, because she never wore underpants with the smock making her available for sex at any time of the day.

When Michael inquired where the new arrivals were located she told him they moved from their first landing spot to a new one approximately six hundred leagues away. It took some time

53

working out the conversion, but they settled on just over eleven hundred kilometers.

Michael went out four hundred meters from their camp and set up early warning sensors tuned for humans, so they would have some warning if they came to the ruins they had been exploring. Kaya advised him that there were Foresters watching the new arrivals. She explained to him that Foresters were individuals who oversaw the wildlife of the planet, and maintained an acceptable level of each species in order that the balance of nature was always maintained. Kaya further explained that each creature she took for food was reported to the Foresters, so they could adjust a population if necessary to replace those taken for food.

They waited for four more days as reports were coming to her that the new arrivals were taking small items, mostly ceramic pieces from the ruins. Michael commented that they were probable for sale on the Black Market to collectors of unique items for their collections.

Late on the fourth day they were told the new people were moving again. In their direction.

They landed and set up camp ten kilometers away from Michael's camp just before dark. Michael was tempted to go visit these people, but Kaya advised him not too. They were safe, and the position of her craft shielded his from sight from that direction.

For two days Michael and Kaya sat watching out towards where the new people were searching through the ruins. Kaya was notified that their footprints had been discovered and that the group of strangers were gathering in what appeared to be a hunt for the origin of those tracks. Michael dressed for battle in his Marine tactical uniform and waited.

When the new comers tripped his outer sensors, Michael told Kaya she was to vanish and not to reveal herself for any reason. He would deal with these people if they discover them, but to reveal herself could give these people the indication there were still people living on this world.

As the first man cleared the edge of the tree line approximately one hundred meters away, Michael dropped his face shield and amplified the view to look at the weapons they were carrying. They were carrying older military weapons often found on developing planets for use by that planets militia units. Obsolete by his standards, but still effective. He knew what he was capable of with his weapons, but was concerned about Kaya and hers.

Kaya had vanished, yet he knew she was near by the feelings he had developed for her. She spoke to him from his left.

"Reach out your left hand and take what I will give you."

He reached out to his left and he felt her hand against his, then something small and hard pressed into his hand. He closed his hand insuring he did not drop what she had given him. Before he could look at the item in his hand, she spoke again.

"Put that to your helmet. It will attach itself and merge with your helmets intelligence. It will allow you to see me via your helmets sensors."

Michael placed it against the rear of his helmet and for a moment he was blind then his visor cleared, and his vision was even sharper than before. He looked to his left and could see Kaya standing with a light blue haze about her telling him she had her cloaking device on.

Seven men cleared the tree line before the first noticed Michael standing next to a tree away from his shuttle. The point man indicated Michael and the men began to spread out as they closed the distance to him. It was then that Michael also saw three other men, shrouded in the same blue haze which covered Kaya and their dress was in tune with hers. These were Foresters following the new comers.

Kaya reached out to his mind.

** "Michael, do you see the Foresters?" **

**" Yes, Kaya I do. If you can, advise them to move to the flanks, and do not get behind these men in case a fight starts." **

Seconds later the Foresters moved to the sides out of the line of fire. Two went left and one went right. Michael could see they were armed like Kaya and carried their weapons ready for a fight.

Michael took two steps away from the tree, so he was more exposed, and had a better view of the men approaching him. Even spread out, they were still bunched close enough together that if they had been one of his Marine Assault Teams, he would have given them a harsh dressing down.

He stood braced for action with his hand on his carbine as it hung in front of him ready to use. Michael let them get within twenty meters before he raised his left hand to indicate for them to stop. He almost laughed as they closed up as they stopped in front of him with several of the men looking around for anyone else that might be in the area. Michael could see the Foresters off to the sides waiting along with Kaya just out of arms reach to his left and slightly forward, but still out of the line of fire from his position.

"What are you people doing here?" He clearly spoke to the gathering in front of him.

"Well soldier boy we are just taking in the fresh air and scenery. What are you doing here? Are you lost or something?" The man who appeared to be their leader spoke.

"No, I'm not lost and what I am doing here is none of your business, but I would suggest you get back on your ship and leave this system in case the frigate I belong too returns today."

"That frigate won't be back today or tomorrow. Maybe next week and we'll be gone long before then. And your shuttle will make for a nice prize for this venture."

"That it might, but you'll never live to see that happen."

"Who are you soldier boy, so we can send notice to your family you died on this empty planet?"

"My name is Senior Lieutenant Michael Conrad Denoyelles, and you can find my family in the Hanover System."

"Well Senior Lieutenant…"

He was interrupted by another member of the group.

"Wait. Did you say you were a Denoyelles from the Hanover System?"

"Mister, I don't like repeating myself, but yes, that's what I said."

The man Michael responded to spoke to the leader.

"I'm out of here Spencer. I'll have no part in killing a Denoyelles."

"What are you talking about Herman?"

"Are you stupid Spencer? Have you been living under a rock? The Denoyelles Family ruled the entire universe at one time and they still are the most powerful family anywhere. We kill him for his shuttle, and the Fleet will hunt us down like rats. The Federation will send the Fleet into this quadrant in force, and sweep everything clean as they move from planet to planet."

"Bullshit Herman. No one is that important especially a soldier."

"Damn you Spencer, he is a Federation Marine by his uniform, and if this was a battle field, his family would accept his death, but not like this. They will come after us without pause."

"Herman, how do you know this?" Spencer asked.

"Because I am from the Hanover System. Lieutenant, what is your relation to the Count?"

"He is my Great-Grandfather. The Duke Denoyelles is my Grandfather. I am often called Baron Denoyelles. Does that answer your question Herman?"

"May the Saints protect us! Spencer, let us leave this world before we are buried here!"

"Herman, why does this one man scare you so much?" Another man from the group asked.

"Five years ago, before I left Hanover, there was a story about the Baron Denoyelles all over the media. He and a small group of men held a line against over a hundred slavers on Esperanto. They say he killed a dozen men with his sword when it came to hand to hand fighting."

"No Herman, I killed fifteen men with my sword that night." Michael interjected.

"Bullshit. If I put a slug in him, he'll die like anyone else." Spencer spoke.

"Spencer, if you raise your rifle to shoot the Baron, I'll kill you myself. It's bad enough living as we do, without being hunted by the entire Fleet." Herman threatened.

Spencer turned to look at Herman, then the other men. Michael could hear a couple of the men softly telling Spencer to back away and leave before it's too late.

"Spencer, I'd take your friends advice and leave. You've violated no crime on this planet that I know of, and any report I make will so state. But if you think you can kill me and take my shuttle, I can promise that all of you will die where you stand."

"One man in the open against seven of us? You are a bold one for sure Denoyelles."

Michael mentally told Kaya to step in front of him, so her cloak would conceal him. She did as he asked and as she centered on him, he grabbed her by the waist and stepped three steps to the right, sat her down and told her to move to the right, exposing him. The effect on the men in front of him was instantaneous.

He was there, then gone, then reappeared to his right in a matter of seconds.

"Do you still think you can win a fight Spencer?" Michael asked.

"Holy Mother of the Saints!" Spencer exclaimed.

Everyone began to back up as no one could believe their eyes. Michael told Kaya to once again cover him which she did as she was watching them. This time Michael just stood watching the men back up even more. He touched his helmet to bring out the tiny boom mic and then amplified his speech through his helmet.

"Do you still think you can win a fight Spencer?" His voice boomed across the distance between him and the men.

They broke and began to run towards the far tree line. Michael could see the Foresters jogging along with them and heard Kaya lightly laugh.

Once the Foresters were in the tree line he took a deep breath, picked Kaya up and walked to the table and chairs at his shuttle, sat her down in a chair, then stepped away as he removed his helmet. Kaya became visible moments later to his unaided eyes.

"Thank you, Kaya."

"For what? You did everything, I just did as you asked."

"You put yourself between them and me. Yes, I asked you to, but you could have refused."

"No, I couldn't Michael."

"Why not?"

"Michael don't you know why?"

"Tell me Kaya. Say the words."

"I did what I did because I have come to love you."

"What do you want from me now Kaya?"

"I want you to take me to your bed and make love to me. Not because of the project, but because it is what I want."

Michael offered his hand to her and she took it. He led her into the shuttle and they lay their weapons and gear on the small table, then as they began to undress, they merged in body and mind.

Kaya awoke alone on Michael's bunk feeling the ache of her first sexual experience and a feeling of contentment in the act. She moved to look around the shuttle to see Michael sitting at his command console looking at the data moving across the main screen. Her hips ached as she moved from being contorted as she was during the act of making love, and she tried not to groan as she sat up.

"How are you feeling Kaya?" Michael asked without looking back at her.

"I feel as if you ruined me, and that I'll never be able to walk normally again." She replied.

"Kaya, is it always going to be like that with us. The way our minds merged and to be lost in the passion of making love?"

"Michael, I've heard of such an effect between lovers. It is rare, but I understand it does happen."

"Okay. Now my sensors show that the scavengers have lifted, but I have no readings as far as their parent craft."

Kaya reached over to the table, retrieved her smock and put her communications bead in her ear. She softly spoke asking for Control, then asked if the space craft was still in orbit. She was informed it was currently boosting out of orbit. Kaya informed Michael of the situation, then replaced the bead back on her smock.

"Kaya, I do have one concern about today. Those men will go back and tell the story about me vanishing, then reappearing in front of them. In time Federation agents will pick up on that story. I can deny it, and no one will challenge me, but it will still raise questions once your people are exposed to the universe. On the up side, it will cause a lot of people to fear having Federation Marines sent to solve problems if the Marines can vanish, then reappear in another location during a battle."

Kaya slowly moved off the bed and stretched before walking to Michael and putting her arms around his neck from behind.

"Michael, was what that man Herman said about you true, or was that another Denoyelles he was talking about?"

"That was me Kaya and what I said to him was also true. I do not wish to talk about that night, but you need to know that it often haunts me at night in my sleep. If you stay in my bed, especially at night, please understand that part of me is not because of you, but because of what happened to me long ago."

"Alright Michael." She kissed him on his cheek then moved away from him.

"I'm going to get dressed and fix us something to eat. We seemed to have missed the mid-day meal and it will be time for the evening meal soon. Do you wish anything special from our larder?"

"Anything will be fine with me Kaya."

As they ate their evening meal, the most either said to one another was when Michael once more complimented Kaya on her preparation of the meal. It was at the end of the meal that Kaya asked a question neither had wanted to broach.

"Michael, what is going to happen between us now?"

Michael put his cup down and looked at her for a moment before answering.

"Kaya, you are the most beautiful woman I have ever known in my life. I am not worthy of your beauty, but I hope we can move forward, together as a couple."

Kaya played with her cup, running a finger around the edge before looking at him as she replied to his comment.

"I'd like that too Michael. But we have other things to also consider. Your uncle will be in orbit in about eight days, and we need to go to the Council and tell them the risk they face."

"Yes, and I had a message when I got up from the Rostislav that they were heading back here. They should be in orbit within four days. When do you suggest we go to the Council?"

"Tomorrow. I'll send a message to them tonight, so they will know we are coming. Michael, we'll have to use your shuttle since mine is not made for two people, especially one as large as you."

"Well, then we had best clean up, stow the table and chairs, then pull down the netting and get it stowed away so we can leave without bother in the morning."

"Yes Michael, that sounds like a good plan."

They spent the rest of the evening getting their camp stowed away, then Kaya sent a message to the capital that they were coming to see the Council in the morning. She secured her vehicle then joined Michael in his small shower before they went to bed.

Michael had adjusted his bunk, so it was large enough for the two of them, but Kaya was draped over him as she went to sleep. He just looked at the ceiling of the moonlit cabin thinking that all else considered, he was the luckiest man alive to have such a woman as Kaya in love with him.

Kaya had used her vehicles AI to research the effect of their mental link during the act of making love. Although it was a rare occurrence, the basis for it was the passion the lovers felt for each other, and the deeper the love for one another, the stronger the psychic tie. The physical effect was more intense than he had ever experienced while making love, draining the body as they were lifted to ecstasy at the end of the physical act.

An Unexpected Turn

Kaya sat beside Michael as he piloted his craft north towards the artic region of the planet. She told him to maintain level flight and speed regardless what he saw in front of him. His faith in her caused him to fly right into a mountain that only existed in the holographic image being used to conceal the city beyond.

The city seen at a distance seemed to be made from alabaster and stainless steel with spirals reaching into the sky. All around the city was the frozen tundra of the region, but within the limits of the city itself, were large portions of green vegetation. The view seemed out of place compared to the rest of the planet with its ruined cities and thick growth of vegetation.

Michael landed his shuttle on a pad on the edge of the city where he noticed a variety of craft neatly parked, ready for use. There was what appeared to be an honor guard waiting for them, which Michael suspected was there to also insure this was not an assault on the capital. Kaya told Michael his sword was acceptable within the capital, but his firearms would have to be left in the shuttle.

One thing he noticed about the honor guard was that their clothing did not reflect the frozen terrain around the city. He checked his shuttle's exterior environmental read-outs and the temperature was pleasant, actually warm as it was 25.5C.

Kaya was wearing her pants with her boots today and Michael was only wearing his basic uniform with battle jacket. His hair was such that his beret would not properly rest on his head, so he just pulled his hair back and tied it, so it would not be in the way. His hair was longer now than it had ever been since entering the service, and as much as Kaya seemed to enjoy running her fingers through the thick mane, he knew he would have to cut it all off once he completed his mission and returned to active duty.

They were placed in a large ground vehicle with another leading and one following as they left the landing field. One thing Michael had quickly noticed was that there did not appear to be any orbital capable crafts on the field. With the technology he had observed, these people should have been out in space decades ago. He figured this was a question he would have to ask Kaya later if he had the chance.

When they arrived at the location where they were to meet with the Council, the guards disembarked and formed a line to the door and saluted them as they walked from the ground car to the main doors of the building, where a distinguished gentleman was standing in front of the open doors.

Kaya was on Michael's left and slipped an arm in his as they walked together. The gentleman gave a slight bow, then stepped aside to indicated they were to enter. Michael suspected this pomp and ceremony was in greeting an off-worlder such as himself, even if he was the first off-worlder to ever enter this building.

Inside, they passed through a lobby, then through another set of doors into a large auditorium. The seating reminded Michael of the theaters on Hanover where standing on the stage, the seating rose so anyone sitting in a seat could see the stage. He estimated that there was enough seating for nearly a thousand people, and the seats were full this morning.

Down they walked at a gentle slope to the stage, where twelve people sat at a large table draped in scarlet cloth. Behind them were large, gold colored drapes with a crimson flag hanging with a multi-colored dragon centered on it. Michael's knowledge of mythology was weak around dragons, but felt the dragon on the flag was of old Earth Asian, instead of medieval European.

Between the stage and the seating was a smaller stage with podium used for addressing the Council. Kaya took Michael to this smaller stage. She reached out to the podium, touched a button and it slowly dropped into the platform so they would not be blocked from view of the Council. Until it was time for him to speak, Kaya handled the introductions.

"Council of Bellus, may I present Baron Michael Denoyelles from the Hanover System of worlds."

Having Kaya introduce him as Baron confused him, but he just stood quietly waiting to be addressed by the Council. He did notice her voice rang through the auditorium for all to hear. The older woman at the center of the Council table stood.

"Baron Denoyelles, the people of Bellus welcomes you. I am Jiazi, Regent of Bellus, and President of the Council. Lady Kaya informs us that you have an important message for the people of Bellus. Please speak so all can hear."

Kaya touched his mind to let him know that the use of Lady was proper for all females.

"Lady Jiazi, Council and People of Bellus, I thank you for your warm greeting. First, I must tell you of my mission to Bellus."

Michael gave a concise briefing on his mission as if he was giving one to his men before an operation. He left nothing out concerning his search of the ruins and the purpose of those searches.

He then gave a brief history of the Centaurian race, so the Council would know about them and his own connection to that race. Then he gave them the warning he felt was correct and proper.

"Council of Bellus. If my being only a quarter Centaurian allows me to open my mind as it has been opened, then I fear what a full-blooded Centaurian can do. They are a warrior race, fierce in battle, and unforgiving when offended. But at the turn of the hand, they are also a warm and caring people to those that respect them, and they respect in return. They can be your most faithful friend, or your worst nightmare of an enemy."

Michael paused to collect his thoughts.

"Unlike the people of Bellus who were left with the technology of these Masters I have heard about, the Centaurians were left to survive with little on a planet wrought with danger, and only their hands to defend themselves with. They survived and developed skills, many as you have from what Lady Kaya has told me, but their racial memory is complete with the struggles to survive."

He paused before he continued to the warning he felt was needed.

"The leader of the expedition to Bellus holds a level of dislike, almost hatred for any person not of the Centaurian race. He is searching for answers which I have no knowledge of, but if he discovers a latent ability to enter another's mind and control them, the universe is at great risk. Humanity is at risk. This must be prevented even at the cost of the lives of the expedition."

The silence within the Council chambers was almost deafening as Michael waited for a response. Lady Jiazi finally broke the silence.

"Baron Denoyelles, some would say you have just committed treason against your own people by your statements. But I believe your ancestor, the Count of Hanover would say otherwise. Yes, Michael Denoyelles, we know some of your history and your ancestors. We have been monitoring communications from other worlds for decades, and have built a large library of information from them. When Lady Kaya identified you, we had our people search for all information concerning you. What we have learned is that you are an honorable human, and I am certain you have given a lot of thought about the effect your warning could have upon your own person. We thank you for the warning."

"Lady Jiazi, my warning comes at no cost to me as I have sworn an oath to protect all people, all races from harm, and I foresee great harm to your race if the Centaurians are successful in discovering their latent psychic abilities. The people of Bellus would still be furless in the eyes of my Uncle, and the laws of Bellus concerning the use of such abilities would not concern him. My uncle is full of hate for his own condition, and believes furless ones are at fault."

"Thank you once again Baron. Now we must address another subject. Lady Kaya, the status of the project?"

"I have mated with Michael, but I am not with child."

"Kaya, are you bonded with the Baron?"

"I tried to bond with him several weeks ago, but he refused the bonding. We have not discussed it since as he made conditions to the mating and bonding at that time."

"I see. Baron Michael Denoyelles. What are your intentions concerning the Lady Kaya?"

"Lady Jiazi, I am not familiar with your culture, and I find the question of my intentions towards Lady Kaya to be between the two of us. Not for public review."

"Baron, our culture does not prevent two people from enjoying each other in an intimate way, but as Kaya's mother, I am interested in the prospect of having you as her bond mate."

Michael could hear Kaya lightly chuckle as she could feel his embarrassment.

"Lady Jiazi, Kaya and I joined not because of the project she has mentioned several times, but because she told me she was in love with me. If she will have me as a husband, I will most certainly have her as my wife."

Kaya stepped away from Michael, drew her sword and laid it across her hands, then stepped back to him and kneeled as was their custom. The words she spoke were similar to those she had spoken earlier with a change in them.

"Michael Denoyelles, I, Kaya Swansea do swear I am yours, body and soul to take as you desire. My sword to you is my bond that I surrender myself as your bond mate, and pledge my love to you and only you."

Michael reached out the took her sword with one hand and held it up from her hands.

"Rise up Kaya Swansea and be known as the Baroness Kaya Denoyelles. Recover your sword and know that in my world, in my culture, you will stand beside me as my wife, not as a bonded mate. Rise, because only slaves live on their knees."

Kaya stood, took her sword from Michael's hand and returned it to its scabbard. He held both hands out to her and she took them as he leaned in and gave her a soft kiss. The auditorium erupted in applause and cheers which was deafening for several minutes. When it once again became quiet, Kaya turned to the Council and waited. Lady Jiazi stood from the Council table.

"Kaya, with the bond being made between you and Baron Denoyelles, the last requirement of your inheritance has been fulfilled. The Council awaits your instructions, Princess Kaya Denoyelles."

Michael was shocked at Kaya being referred to as Princess. He still had ahold of her right hand as they stood looking at the Council.

"Mother, it is my wish and desire that you continue to sit as Regent to the Throne of Bellus and govern in my stead, as I still have so much to finish with the project, and to learn from my husband, the Baron."

"Kaya, I accept your appointment and with the Council's approval, I shall remain Regent until you decide to ascend the throne. How does the Council vote on this?"

One by one the Council voted 'yea' to the question put to them. Lady Jiazi accepted the vote then turned her attention back to the newlyweds before her.

"Baron Michael Denoyelles. Because of your genetic profile being equal to our own, and because you are of royal blood from your home world, you are hereby known of Baron Denoyelles, Prince of Bellus, consort to the throne of Bellus."

Lady Jiazi picked up what Michael recognized as a polished stone and rapped it had on a piece of hardwood which caused it to ring throughout the auditorium. The Council stood and bowed to them, and Michael heard a noise behind him and looked over his shoulder to see all the people in the auditorium standing and bowing.

Lady Jiazi rose, and once again struck the stone.

"This meeting is hereby adjourned."

Kaya turned and took Michael's hand and began leading him from the chambers. No one in the auditorium spoke or moved as they walked hand in hand out of the auditorium. In the lobby area Michael finally spoke.

"Where are we going now Kaya?"

"We are going to my quarters, and to my bed to consummate our bonding."

"Kaya, on my world we called in a wedding or marriage ceremony."

"Then husband, we are going to consummate our marriage to one another."

Michael had trouble believing the opulence of Kaya's apartment. He had been in the Hanover Castle and had seen his ancestor's living quarters, but Kaya's were far above Conrad Denoyelles' apartment. He stopped in the public area of her quarters and just looked around at all the fine fabrics, precious metals and stones adorning the apartment.

When she pulled on him to take him into her sleeping quarters he held fast, refusing to move.

"Kaya, I accept your secrets as you accept mine. But this is far above what I have seen of you since we met. Would you care to explain to your confused husband?"

"Michael, I guess first all I need to explain that the royal aspect is because of the Masters. They created my bloodline to lead before they left according to our history. My father was a scientist who found himself on the throne after his elder brother, the Prince was killed while working as a Forester. Yes Michael, the throne is a governing part of life here, but not a way of life."

"If your father is dead, why didn't your mother assume the throne as Princess, instead of being the Regent to the throne?"

"I'm sure you noticed her hair. Only the royal line has hair such as mine. It is an indicator to all who is of royal blood. I am the last of the line since my mother was a commoner. If our child has the silver of hair, they will stand in line behind me for the throne."

"What is your field of endeavor?"

"Michael, I am trained as a Forester. I love the outdoors and the animals, even the vicious bera which killed my uncle. My father discovered the cause of our decline in population and had worked out the possible cure. I was never part of his research, but when he died from the stress of his work on his heart, I stepped in as I felt it was my place as heir to the throne. But according to our custom, no royal can ascend to the throne unless they are bonded to another, married as you state. I would have given myself to any man who we felt could provide my people with the genetic infusion to save us, regardless of the outcome and never ascend to the throne."

Michael could only admire her dedication to save her people.

"Kaya, then it was fate that we met and fell in love."

"Call it what you will my darling, as long as you get out of that uniform and take me to my, excuse me, our bed."

Kaya was already undressing as she spoke, and Michael knew there was no way he could deny her, wedding day or not. For a moment as he was undressing, a thought entered his mind and stuck there for later review as he was not about to get side tracked from attending to Kaya.

Later as Michael lay beside Kaya resting from a second bout of sexual combat, he remembered the thought that had entered his mind. He eased out of bed and as he was dressing, Kaya awoke.

"Michael, are you going somewhere?"

"Honey, what are my powers, how much authority do I have as Prince of Bellus?"

"Not much of any until I ascend the throne. Why?"

"Not a problem, but get up and get dressed. We are going to the shuttle, so I can send a message which should slow things down as far as the exploration team is concerned. And dress nice, it has been said a photo is worth a thousand words."

Kaya eased out of bed and went to her closet where she removed a nice outfit to wear. The smock was crimson with the dragon embroidered over the left breast and the trousers were silver like her hair.

She thought it would be nice to bath first after being so sweaty from their love making, but he was in a hurry to do whatever was on his mind, and she was not going to slow him down. She put on silver slippers then brushed out her long hair as he finished dressing.

"Kaya, we are going to need a ride to the shuttle."

"There will be a vehicle outside for us to use Michael."

"Good. I'm ready, shall we go?"

A Long Distance Call

When they exited the building, Michael found himself looking at a large ground vehicle with livered driver and guards. There was no actual formality between Kaya and the entourage awaiting her as she just climbed into the back of the vehicle and sat down. When the driver asked for their destination, Kaya just stayed quiet putting Michael in command of the situation. Michael told the driver to take them to his shuttle and the only response was yes sir.

At the shuttle, he told the driver to wait then he guided Kaya into the vehicle and secured the door behind them. As he sat at the command console setting up for his long-distance communications, he asked Kaya about the entourage and the vehicle. She told him it came with the title, but it could be adjusted.

"Is there a need to have that many armed guards here at the capital?"

"No Michael, it's more of a tradition than a requirement plus the men are employed. We've never needed an armed force, but they are more an honor guard then actually security although they are well trained in all their weapons."

"Do I have any say so concerning the guards?"

"Certainly, my love, they are yours to command."

"Okay, I'll discuss this more with you later, but for the moment, come and stand by me as I make this call."

Kaya stood patiently next to Michael as his signal found its destination. His monitor split into two screens and the first individual she saw was a gentleman who had a heavy beard over his face.

"Michael, how is the survey going?"

"Fine father, but if you will give me a minute, I'm trying to link Grand-Father into this conversation."

A smile came upon his father's face as he could see Kaya in the background, but never said a word as he waited. A few moments later the second screen showed a much older man with very distinguished looks.

"Michael, it is good to see you, and I see a lovely young lady near. Care to explain why you have myself and your father on the line at the same time, and using a restricted channel?"

"Grand-Father, Father may I introduce my wife, the Princess Kaya of Bellus. But before you ask where Bellus is located, it is known to the Federation as N61358."

Michael went on to explain how they met and what had happened since his landing on the planet. He never got into their ability to conceal themselves or their psychic abilities, but he did tell them these people had memories of the same people that had taken the Centaurians from Earth.

"Grand-Father, I have learned things about the people of Bellus that must not become known to the universe. I cannot explain right now, but I would have it made known to the Federation that I am declaring Planet N61358, also known as Bellus to be quarantined under the Unknown Alien Species Act, which Grand-Father Conrad had placed into the Federation Charter."

"Michael, your Uncle Abraham will soon be in orbit and will not take this lightly." His Grand-father spoke.

"Grand-Father, he is the very reason I am placing Bellus under quarantine."

"Have you sent the order out yet to the Fleet?" His father asked.

"No Sir, but unless either of you can determine I am wrong in this, I was going to send the message out once we break contact."

"Son, the Federation Charter states that the Senior surveying officer can declare a quarantine at any time during the survey without specific reason at the time of the order. From that moment, the quarantine is in effect for sixty solar days of issuance before valid cause must be given, or the quarantine will expire."

"I'm aware of the time frame Father. I need that time to find a reason to keep everyone off the planet so the Bellusarians can be protected unlike the Centaurians were. I cannot say anymore right now about this, but please trust me in this."

His Grand-Father redirected the conversation to Kaya.

"I would like to know what my Grand-Daughter in Law has to say about this. Princess Kaya, do you support Michael's plan?"

"Yes Grand-Father Denoyelles, I do."

"What does your father have to say, or does he know of Michael's plan."

"Sir, my father is dead. I sit on the throne of Bellus."

Kaya lied about her current position on the throne, but felt Michael needed all the support possible with his plan. She completed her support of Michael.

"Sir, may I say that Baron Michael Denoyelles is also known to the population of Bellus as Prince Michael Denoyelles. As I stand by his side as his wife, he stands by my side as ruler of Bellus. He has met the people of Bellus, and they have accepted him in due form."

"Michael, there is your key to keeping Abraham and his researchers off Bellus. The rulers of a newly discovered planet can restrict access of that planet to all Federation personal until a formal treaty between said planet, and the Federation can be made, and approved by the Federation Congress." His Grand-Father offered.

Michael was quiet as he mentally told Kaya what she needed to say next.

"Duke Denoyelles, I formally request that you represent the Throne of Bellus in all negotiations between Bellus and the Federation. Will you accept the Thrones request?"

"Princess Kaya of Bellus, I hereby accept the position as representative for Bellus to the Federation Council and Congress. This communication is being recorded and will be edited to show your request and my acceptance of the request. It will show that the Earl Thomas Denoyelles as a witness. What are your instructions your Highness?"

"If I may speak for my wife, the Princess. Grand-Father, I would think that your ship in orbit with Grand-Mother Ireesha at the quickest possible date would be advantageous to our situation here on the ground. Please bring my Father and Mother so they can meet their new Daughter-in-Law."

"Prince Michael of Bellus, so it shall be as soon as arrangements can be made. We will send a message to your shuttle when we boost from Hanover once your parents can ship over from Denoyelles. May I suggest that you include my position in this when you submit your message to the Federation concerning quarantine."

When the link was broken between Michael and his ancestors, he formulated the message to the Federation and the Fleet in accordance to the advice he had been given. He had Kaya read it since she now understood both the written and spoken language of the Federation. She asked for only a minor adjustment in the message, then told Michael to send it.

Kaya sighed once the message was sent and went back to the bed and just sat on it.

"What's wrong Kaya?"

"I gave my Mother the Regency because I felt I did not have time to ascend the throne, and here I just became the crown even for a few minutes. Michael, I have to tell my mother about this."

"Kaya, I will take the blame for this since I did not brief you beforehand, and my Grand-Father pushed the issue without knowledge of your status on the throne."

"No Michael. I could have told your Grand-Father the truth of my reign, but felt you were right, and it is my place to support you as you try to protect our people. No, I will accept her judgement."

When they reentered the ground vehicle, Michael quickly learned that the building Kaya's apartment was located was call the Cathedral. She walked with him to the door to her apartment, kissed him, then left him to enter alone while she went to see her mother.

It was nearly an hour before Kaya returned and she told Michael that her mother would say that she had talked to them before they made the call to his parents, and that she gave approval for Kaya to request the assistance of the Denoyelles family. Kaya also said if she did something like this again, her mother would step down from the Regency, and require her to take the throne.

Kaya then took Michael into her bath and they took a long, hot soaking bath before turning in for the night. Even though she was upset at being put in the position she was, by pretending to be the Throne of Bellus, she was very aggressive in their love making this night.

Reaction Mass

They spent another day at the capital before returning to the ruins where her vehicle was located. Michael had over a dozen messages when he entered the shuttle. He ignored them except the message that his family had boosted from orbit around Hanover and were enroute to Bellus. Estimated date of arrival was twenty-two days.

Once on the ground, Kaya went about resetting their camp with additional items brought from the capital. One was a larger refrigeration unit which was lightweight and folded out under its own servos. Kaya had it hooked into her vehicles power cell, then stocked it with the things packed in ice for the trip.

Michael went through the messages which he found included a copy of his Grand-Father's notice to the Federation that he had been retained as the representative to the Federation for, and by the Throne of Bellus.

He also had acknowledgements from the Federation of his notice of quarantine with instructions to the Frigate Rostislav to enforce the quarantine until either relieved of duty by another Fleet vessel, or by the removal of the quarantine by Captain Michael Denoyelles, Fleet Marine Force, surveyor of Bellus. This was the first clue that he had been promoted to Captain.

The one message he waited to read until last was from his Uncle Abraham demanding to know the reason of the quarantine. He was not aware of the reasons Michael had given the Federation, only that Michael had closed the planet to exploration.

Michael responded to Abraham's message with only an acknowledgement of its receipt. Michael figured once Abraham did not receive an explanation, he would be a terror on the Institute's ship because of his temper.

Kaya called him to the mid-day meal where she served a hunk of porcine with vegetables and a light wine. He told her about the messages and the time frame for his parents to arrive. When she asked him what he intended to do until they arrived, he said he was going to continue his assignment in searching the ruins.

Kaya asked him exactly what he was looking for in the ruins and he showed her the briefing packet. She laughed and told him that everything he was looking for was back at the capital based upon the symbols given. Kaya said some of that information was the basis for their invisibility programs.

When he asked what the symbols meant, she told him the symbols was the writing of the Masters. They were the laboratory symbols on the work they were doing based on what the Bellus history told them. The Masters had left the planet in their ships leaving everything intact for the people to use to take care of themselves.

She told him that according to the history of the Masters, there were two planets where humans were being studied and research done on them to hopefully save the Masters race. There was Zyra and Bellus. The information on Zyra was incomplete, but it was the first research location.

According to what the Bellusarians have been able to reconstruct from the records, the Masters released their test subjects into the wilds of the planet with just enough skills to survive after destroying the laboratories and other facilities. From what they understood was, this was part of the final test, to see if the modified humans could survive and grow.

Michael told Kaya that the subjects on Zyra did in fact grow a population which was almost destroyed by the introduction of Earth normal humans, until laws were set into place to protect them. It is those laws, and even newer laws he was using to protect the Bellusarians from encroachment.

Kaya then asked if there were laws to prevent others from landing on Bellus, why did he ask for his ancestors to come when they could communicate without contact. Michael smiled as he answered.

"First of all, no one will attempt to ignore the quarantine with the personal ship of the Duke Denoyelles in orbit, especially since he will be acting as representative of the Bellus throne. Not even my Uncle Abraham, who is related by marriage to the Duke."

"Second there will be an Altairian doctor aboard that ship. The Altairian's were noted for their genetic research. Hopefully they will become interested in what is happening here and help."

Michael told the story of Duke Conrad Denoyelles wife, the Duchess Jilena Denoyelles who had problems during her first pregnancy which was discovered to be a genetic defect. The Altairians were able to correct the defect which allowed Jilena to have more children including his Grand-Father.

Kaya was quiet for a long time as she considered what he had told her.

"Yes Michael, an Altairian physician could be of great help. The reason for our population decline is a genetic one which we have not been able to solve here on Bellus. The risk of miscarriage has been high along with the deaths of the mother. Our population expanded for a millennium then began to decline. My father said it was because the lack of diversity in the genetic profile of our people was the cause of the medical problems in bringing forth new children. Therefore, we needed you or someone like you to infuse new genetic material into our population."

"Kaya, are you saying that you stand a high risk of dying while pregnant because of this genetic defect?"

"Yes Michael, I am."

"Then why are you risking your life in such a manner? Why haven't your government gone out into the universe to seek help?"

"I am the hereditary ruler of Bellus. It is my place to put myself at risk for my people. I could not, cannot ask another to take such a risk. And as for going out to seek help, we have been secluded for so long, we did not know what humanity had evolved into during our seclusion. We have monitored communication signals for decades, and some of what we have heard terrified us."

"Yes Kaya, I have no doubt what you have heard was terrifying considering your lack of contact with the rest of humanity. We are a violent people otherwise there would be no need for men like me."

"Michael, I have been inside you, seen your true self. You despise what you do even though you never hesitate to go out and do those things for humanities sake. I have seen your nightmares as we slept, and felt the anguish inside of you for what you were doing. Because of the link between our minds before you took me to your bed, I witnessed things I could never imagine and felt your pain. It is one of the reasons I fell in love with you Michael."

She paused and reached out to take his hands.

"We saw the evil in those you call slavers and how they never felt remorse for what they were doing. But you fight against those people, and even as you try to remove their type from the universe, you hate the actions required of you. I pray to my ancestors that you find peace here on Bellus."

Michael was quiet during the rest of the meal and after he helped clean up after the meal he asked to be left alone as he walked out into the forest and just wandered as he thought about what she had told him concerning the risk to her person in becoming pregnant. The genetic defect was within her own genetic make-up and for the first time in his life, he had found someone who loved him as much as he loved her.

The thought of losing her terrified him but he had to respect her position concerning solving the problem of her people. It was possible she was already with child as often as she gave herself to him. His own desires to make love to her placed her at risk without his knowledge and he was angry that the fact regardless of how he felt about the situation, he could not deny her desires to be with him or to hopefully help her people.

For once in his life he could not fight against what was in front of him. His one hope was that the Altairians could find a cure ahead of the Bellusarians' own project and that he would not lose

Kaya or a child because he could not and would not deny her the possibility of helping her people.

Michael thought about his ancestor, the last Count of Hanover, Duke Conrad Denoyelles and how in his autobiography had told of risk he took, and how he never figured on living to see his dreams come true. He had placed himself at risk to insure the rest of the Hanover System was free of a system which basically made slaves of the people with royalty as masters. Not only had Conrad Denoyelles changed that system, he ultimately changed the universe.

He sat under a large tree for hours considering his own family history and recognized they were cursed in that they continued the work of Conrad even at the risk of their own lives as he had. Michael hated the things he had done in the name of the Fleet and the Federation which his ancestor had changed. Changed for the betterment of humanity, but there was still much work to do, and he was beginning to wonder if he had what it took to continue that work.

Michael lost track of time until he felt Kaya touch his mind and remind him he had to eat. He had to get his bearing as he had completely lost track of his location as he wandered thinking about the situation he had found himself in. He returned just in time as Kaya was taking steaks off the firepit that came from a deer like creature found in the forest. He sat down at his place at the table and waited as she finished setting things up then sat down.

"Kaya, how many Foresters are there in the area watching us?"

"Ten."

"Why are they here?"

"Lord Titus, who oversees the Foresters assigned them for our protection."

"Does Titus think I cannot protect you?"

"Michael, please, he means well."

"Alright. This is your world, not mine, so I guess I had best get used to this sort of thing."

"Michael, what's wrong?"

"You mean you cannot see what's wrong?"

"No, because I will not look into your mind to discover your pain. Please talk to me."

Michael moved a few vegetables around on his plate as he considered her statement.

"Kaya, I'm scared of losing you because of my desire to be with you. At the same time, I cannot refuse you. For once in my life I have no answers or guidance to solve this problem. This is unlike combat where the enemy is obvious, and the job is out in the open."

"Michael, the only thing about what I am doing is that we love each other. If you had taken me the first time I offered, and I had become pregnant, I would have left you to return to the capital without you knowing my condition, or the conditions I was facing. I'm also scared my love that I have created my own demise. But I am duty bound, much like you are to your Marines, to see this project through the best I can. If fate decides against us, let's make the most of the time we have together."

"I will give you what you desire because I love you, and understand the duty which you have taken for your people. In many ways, you are well suited to carry the Denoyelles name in marriage. I have a book I wish you to read. It is the story of my ancestor who changed the universe, and his struggles and fears. It is a weight all who carry the Denoyelles name must bear."

"I will read it Michael because I wish to know you better, and hopefully survive this project and teach our children about your ancestors, as I will instruct them of mine."

The Rostislav settled into orbit that evening and contacted Michael to let him know they were on station and understood their orders concerning the quarantine. His Uncle Abraham was due in orbit within three days and was sending messages every few hours demanding answers to the quarantine preventing him from landing with his research team. Michael only acknowledged receipt of the messages, but never responded to them.

Michael did notice that at no time in the messages from Abraham was the mention of Kaya or the Bellusarian people, which meant that his Grand-Father was keeping that a secret at the time. Whomever his Grand-Father had contacted at the Federation level was also maintaining the knowledge of the Bellusarians a secret until Grand-Father arrived in orbit.

That evening Michael had problems relaxing and making love to Kaya until she eased into his mind, and gave him the calm he needed. Unlike many nights where their love making was wild and exhausting, tonight it was slow and fulfilling for both of them.

After the morning meal was complete and the table was cleared, Michael told Kaya to call in all the Foresters, so he could talk with them. Kaya asked him why and he told her he had his reasons and to trust him. She sent out the message to include his instructions that once at the camp, everyone was to make themselves visible to the naked eye. He also had her shut down the cloaking device on her personal vehicle, so it would be visible to sensors from orbit.

Michael's plan had the desired result as Kaya's vehicle and she became visible to the sensors on the Rostislav. When he had brought his shuttle back to the camp, he had guided it so that the rear ramp would open just inside the cloak of Kaya's vehicle thus keeping her invisible when outside around the camp.

In the Sensor Department of the Rostislav, the duty operators thought something had gone wrong with their sensors, and were running test after test to determine why suddenly another person, then a vessel suddenly appeared on their screens. Then one, two and as many as three humans appeared by just popping up on their screens until they had a count of twelve people, and an unknown vehicle at the shuttle.

Once the Rostislav realized their equipment was not malfunctioning, they contacted Michael to inquire about the additional personal and vehicle at his campsite. Michael's response was short and simple. The additional individuals at his camp was the reason for the quarantine.

When Abraham received the information concerning the new people with Michael, he demanded a video conference with him to discuss this new development. Michael ignored the request as he had other things on his mind.

Michael stood before seven men and three women in their Forester uniforms and addressed them.

"Foresters, I understand that you have been assigned as our guardians by Lord Titus. I will not intrude on his authority or the customs of your world. But understand this, you will remain visible at all times, so I know where you are located as you accomplish your mission. I am also going to have five Federation Marines brought down from our ship in orbit to team up with you. Two Foresters per one Marine. I am doing this, so they can evaluate your abilities, and if need be train you to the standards I am familiar with. If you prove to be superior in ability to those Marines, then I expect you to train them. Are there any questions?"

One of the females raised her hand.

"Yes, and your name please."

"My name is Virna. Your sword is shaped very different from ours, I was wondering about its strength."

Michael smiled and reached over his shoulder and pulled the katana from its scabbard. He walked over to a tree that he could not put his hands around, then signaled for Virna to join him at the tree.

"Virna, take a single cut at the tree about chest high. I wish to see how well your sword cuts before I demonstrate mine."

Michael stepped back out of her way as she drew her sword, took a good stance, then took a two-handed swing at the tree with her sword. It cut just over halfway through the tree trunk and stuck her sword making it unable for her to remove it.

He had her step away, looked at the gathering watching this demonstration, pivoted as he swung with one hand and hit the tree below Virna's sword, slicing completely through the tree with ease. The comments between the Foresters were ones of amazement at what they had witnessed.

"Prince Denoyelles, where did you get such a blade?" One of the men asked.

"Your name sir?"

"Jimni sir."

"Well Jimni, my sword was made by a craftsman that is somewhat related to you. There is a race called the Centaurians which I have told the Council that were also taken from Earth by the Masters. One of their sword masters forged this blade for me as a gift. One other thing Foresters, do not refer to me as Prince, especially once the Marines arrive. Only use the title Captain. There are secrets we must keep from the Marines and the Federation Fleet for the time being."

The group acknowledged the order.

"Another thing. At no time are you to use your cloak, to include the ones on your vehicles. This is a secret we must keep from the Fleet at all costs. When the Marines arrive, as they are assigned to pairs, they will stay with you at all times, including sleeping at or near your vehicles. So, we do not need them discovering the cloak. The Fleet is already confused by your appearing here, this will further require them to ask questions we are not ready to answer right now. I want each of you to bring your vehicles and park them inside the far tree line spaced about one hundred meters apart, and make them visible before you leave their current location. Go, we have work to do."

After the Foresters had left to fulfill their instructions, Kaya questioned him about his plan.

"Michael is it wise to bring those Marines down, and introduce them to the Foresters?"

"I've given this a lot of thought and to be honest I am not sure, but I know those Marines that will be coming down here, and they will keep what they see and hear a secret because of me. I have served with them on distant planets during hard times. I trust them with my life and now your life, but I want to insure the people protecting us are as capable as those Marines. And if the Marines learn from your Foresters, then that is a plus for all concerned."

Michael went into the shuttle and contacted the Rostislav. He informed the Marine Detachment Commander that he wanted Senior Sergeant McKenzie along with four other Marines of McKenzie's choosing to come down for an indefinite period as a security detail.

It was also during this time that the Foresters began to uncloak their vehicles and move them according to Michael's instructions. The Rostislav stopped inquiring after the third vehicle uncovered and Michael told the Rostislav to ignore what they were seeing. Once on the ground, the Foresters once more gathered at Michael's camp to await further instructions.

Two hours later Michael was notified that the detail was shipping down to his location. As they made a pass over of the open field next to Michael's shuttle, they found him standing in the middle of the field as a marker where to land. The landing was smooth with McKenzie at the controls of their armored, assault vehicle.

Kaya had brought up the fact there would be a language problem between the Marines and the Foresters, and that the Foresters could not meld with Marines as she had done with him. He asked about the device which she had given him, so he could see her while cloaked and she said it should work if the Marines were wearing their helmets.

She gathered up five of the buttons as Michael referred to them, and reprogramed them in her vehicle to only translate which would give the Marines a start at learning the Bellusarian language.

It was then that Michael came to realize he had been speaking Bellusarian all the time he was talking to the Foresters. Kaya said he had been using her language for several days, and she just thought he was trying to assimilate into her culture.

Michael greeted each man as they disembarked the shuttle and told them to attach the button to their battle helmet. He briefed the men on why he had them come to the surface and told them what he expected from them. Not only did they know of Michael's promotion to Captain, they brought his new rank insignia with them.

He told them once he had them teamed up, they were to move their personal gear to a location near the Foresters vehicles and make camp with them. The Marines understood what he was doing as they had worked with militias in similar ways to get them up to standards.

Kaya has expressed a concern that the females in the group would join with the male Marines at night. Michael asked if that was prohibited to which Kaya said no, but the risk of pregnancy may be a problem. As Kaya was quietly talking to the female Foresters about the risk, Michael was talking to the Marines telling them that if the situation did arise, to insure from their end of the joining the females could not become pregnant.

Michael had to admit that all of the Bellusarian females he had seen were attractive, but Kaya was far above the rest in body and looks. When he took the Marines into camp, he had to smile to himself that the Marines seemed to focus on Kaya instead of the other females since she was dressed as they were.

The Foresters were lined up and Kaya moved to Michael's side and took his hand letting the Marines know she was not part of the deal. What Michael was not aware of at the moment, was that Kaya had chain linked with the Foresters and transferred her knowledge of Michael's language to them, so they could at least understand the Marines.

Michael was not going to make things complicated any more so than they already were, so he just made the introductions and assigned two Foresters to a Marine insuring the three females were paired with a male Forester, so a Marine would not have two females to deal with.

Once the teams were set, he introduced Kaya as his wife and they discovered she spoke very good Federation speak. Michael instructed the teams to get the Marines gear off loaded and their team camps established. Movement of the Forester vehicles was allowed as long as they maintained the alignment already established. Team camps would be between the two vehicles belong to a team.

After the team camps were established, he wanted a sensor perimeter set out at five hundred meters from his shuttle. Senior Sergeant McKenzie took matters in his own hands and moved the Marine assault boat next to the tree line in the center of the Forester line. The assault boat was equipped with two full body sanitizers which they would have to use during their stay on the planet. McKenzie showed the Foresters how to access the boat and warned them to stay out of the command section of the boat since they could set off the boat's weapons systems by mistake.

The Foresters shifted their crafts, then the teams set up their individual camps. All but one team set up a single shelter before setting out to set the sensor line. This was the Foresters first lesson. How to deal with the sensors used by the Federation. The Foresters were aware that their cloaking devices could defeat the sensors, but Michael had them add the small buttons which would now give the sensors the ability to see through the cloaks in case someone tried to sneak in that should not be there.

The rest of the day for the Marines were in giving their team members a complete review of the gear they carried and its purpose. The Foresters went through their belt gear leaving out that their communications device also had the cloaking device incorporated into it. Weapons were compared and when the Foresters asked why they did not carry swords, they had to explain the Captain Denoyelles carried his as part of his heritage, but it was not part of Marine issue.

The next day the Marines set up a firing range to test their teams on the use of their weapons. At close range, the Foresters were on par with the Marines, but as the distance increased, they began to miss more than they hit. Senior Sergeant McKenzie examined the Forester weapons and determined they were not made for distance, but for close-in self-defense.

Michael contacted the Rostislav and requested weapons for the Foresters under his title of Baron instead of Captain. He knew that he might get some flak for doing so as a Captain, but no one would question the request from the Baron Denoyelles. Weapons, ammunition and maintenance equipment, plus spare parts were dropped using a drone resupply vehicle which would have to be picked up by a crewed shuttle later in the mission.

Sergeant McKenzie then set about training the Foresters on the new weapons and how to use them. With the new weapons, the Foresters proved to be excellent shots at long distances and on an equal standing with the Marines. In turn, the Foresters requested swords for the Marines after they checked each Marine with their personal swords for length and balance. Training swords were also brought in and they spent one hour a day training with the swords.

Michael was watching the Marines training with the swords when his remote communicator announced he had a priority message. Kaya entered the shuttle with him, but stayed out of the view of the camera as he answered the call. He knew before opening who would be at the other end of the call.

"What can I do for you Doctor Kerekes?" He addressed his Uncle by his university name.

"What in the name of the seven saints are you doing down there, Captain Denoyelles?" Abraham's anger was obvious.

"I'm surveying Bellus, formally known as N61358 as per my mission orders Sir." Michael kept a calm voice knowing it would further upset his uncle.

"Captain Denoyelles. As the head of this expedition, I order you to remove the quarantine immediately, so my team can go down to the surface and began our research."

"Sorry Doctor Kerekes, I cannot do that. I do not work for you, I work for the Fleet Marines which means I am oath sworn to not only follow the laws of the Federation, but to enforce them."

"You quarantine the planet, then have five Marines sent down to your location! How is that a quarantine?"

"Doctor Kerekes, by Fleet regulations, I am authorized security personal during a survey of a new planet. I exercised that right when I asked for the Marines. I followed regulations Sir. If I had requested the Marines to come to the surface without said regulations on my side, the Marine Detachment Commander, and the Captain of the Rostislav would have counter-manned my request, and said Marines would still be in orbit."

"From what I have been told by my ships sensor technicians is that there are more than you and five Marines at your location. Who are these people, and by what right do you have to do what you have done by preventing me from going down to the surface?"

Kaya stepped out from behind the divider from the command center to the cabin and stopped next to Michael. Michael could see her in his screen knowing that Abraham could also see her.

"Doctor Kerekes, Captain Denoyelles has issued the quarantine upon the request of the Bellus government. Until we can establish diplomatic relations with the Federation, no one can land except those authorized by the Council of Bellus."

"And just who are you little girl?" Abraham's anger was getting the better of him.

"I am Princess Kaya Swansea Denoyelles. Heir to the throne of Bellus, and wife of Baron Michael Denoyelles of Hanover. I give you this warning Doctor Kerekes, any attempt to land on Bellus without either the Council's approval, or Captain Denoyelles approval will be met with force. Do you understand my instructions Doctor Kerekes?"

"What kind of joke is this Michael?" Abraham asked.

"Uncle Abraham, this is not a joke, and beware of insulting my wife again or I will forget that you are blood kin and meet you with cold steel. The Princess Kaya has issued her instructions, I would take care to obey them."

"This will ruin your career Michael."

"It will be what it will be. I think we are done here now."

"Michael, wait……"

Michael broke the connection and leaned back in his command chair. Kaya put her hand on his shoulder and spoke to him.

"Michael, I could not stand back and watch him berate you in such a manner."

Michael put his hand on hers.

"Darling, I am used to Uncle Abraham treating me as an inferior, but notice how angry he was becoming. I was hoping that he would show his true self, but your stepping in gave him pause to cool some before he stepped over the line."

"How did he insult me Michael?"

"His use of the term little girl was his way of saying you were unimportant in the scheme of things. It was meant to demean you, diminish your importance in his eyes. He will not make that mistake again, especially once my Grand-Mother, his sister arrives."

"What now Michael?"

"The security teams will prevent any interference from outsiders as we continue to survey the planet. I am aware that most likely everything they are searching for is at the capital, but I must follow through with my orders. If I stop, then Abraham can use that against me later unless the Fleet orders me to cease or suspend the survey. I must do my duty Kaya."

"Then I will assist you in your duties until it is known that I am with child and can no longer go into the field with you."

"Kaya, I am still concerned about your safety if becoming pregnant has become such a high risk for your people."

"Michael, I believe you would be concerned even if you did not love me. But this is a path I must walk, and I think having you by my side will make the trip worth the trouble."

Kaya's Decision

Kaya was moody for the next several days after her statement to Abraham. Michael did not pry into her reason for being moody and gave her all the room she needed, or the attention she required. He was wondering if she was pregnant and this was one of the effects of her condition.

Five days after she had given Abraham her ultimatum, Kaya told Michael she was going back to the Capital. He asked her if she thought she was pregnant, to which she replied that she was going to assume the throne since she was acting like the leader of this world when dealing with off-worlders. Her own conscious required her to assume the throne and allow her mother to follow her own path.

Michael asked if she wanted him to go with her she told him no since she had to leave cloaked, so no one in orbit would know where the capital may be located. Michael gave her a kiss and told her to fly safely and return as soon as she could because he would miss her.

Kaya cloaked her vehicle before lifting off giving the Rostislav techs fits once again. The Rostislav Captain had ordered the Hawkins Institute ship to take a much higher orbit, and not to use their sensors to scan the planet as part of the quarantine, so they never saw Kaya's ship blink out on their screens.

Jiazi met her daughter when she landed near the Cathedral.

"Kaya, why have you returned alone?"

"Mother, I found myself in a position which I could not avoid and stepped into the role of the leader of Bellus. I am here to take the throne, and make myself legitimate in such dealings with off-worlders."

"Are you referring to the newest vessel in orbit?"

"Yes Mother. That ship is the Hawking's Institute from the world we know as Zyra. Michael's uncle is the leader of the expedition, and he was verbally violent towards Michael when it was discovered that Michael had placed Bellus under quarantine."

"Michael placed Bellus under quarantine? Why?"

"Mother, he explained all of that during the meeting with the Council. I support his reasoning and would even if we were not mated."

"Alright then. I'll summon the Council and make your ascension to the throne official."

"Mother, I do need you to stay on the Council to be my voice while I am away with my husband."

"Husband? You have adopted his manners already."

"Mother, I like the terms husband and wife. They seemed to have a greater meaning to him than mate, even a bonded mate. It puts me as his equal in his eyes."

"But Kaya you are a Princess while he is a Baron. You are above him in status."

"Mother, no person is above him except his ancestors. And they even talk to him as an equal. It is the nature of his people, and it is one I think we can respect."

"As you wish my daughter. Shall we go and make the transfer of the throne to you a reality?"

Two hours later Kaya was formally the ruler of Bellus and her mother was titled as Chancellor to the Throne, giving her a seat on the Council while Kaya was in the field with her husband.

Kaya explained what was happening in space above them and the efforts of Michael in preventing what he considered a potential disaster if the Centaurians were to land and discover they had a latent talent which would make them a very powerful political race.

Once the Council had adjourned, she went to the physicians and was tested to determine if she was with child. The test returned with a positive reading. She asked the physician to keep this a secret for a time, then told her mother the same.

When Kaya returned to the camp Michael asked if she had been to see the doctor. Kaya had worked hard to conceal her feelings on the way to be with Michael, and lied as she told him she was not yet with child. He told her to be patient it would come in time. He also told her that Virna had come to him to announce that she had assumed the Throne of Bellus, since it had been broadcast to everyone in their different positions in the field.

Kaya hated lying to Michael, but she knew he would worry about her, and she didn't want that burden on him with her pregnancy right now.

The In-Laws

Michael spent his time just walking in the forest searching for anything that might constitute ruins, so he could justify staying in one position. He finally had to admit defeat and moved to another ruined city to search it.

It made for an interesting move with Michael's shuttle in the lead with the Marines Assault Boat next and the Foresters flying on either flank to their new campsite. This time the security teams spread out around the perimeter of the camp giving coverage from any direction. This was Sergeant McKenzie's idea as a way to teach tactics to the Foresters. It also gave McKenzie more privacy as he had been sleeping with Elpidia, the female on his team.

One team always monitored the sensors from the assault boat while the others patrolled, or provided security for Michael and Kaya as they explored the ruined city. He filed daily reports with copies now going up to the Institute ship.

Sergeant Norby, who was second in command was injured while on patrol when a bera charged out of the underbrush and caught him off guard. His two teammates killed the bera and brought it into camp later to provide meat to the teams. Norby wasn't seriously injured, but was restricted to monitoring the sensors until his wounds healed.

Michael had never seen a bera, but recognized it as the small ceramic statue he had found and used to set a booby-trap for Kaya. The bera was a six-legged version of a black bear with this one going just over two hundred kilos. The meat was red, and had a taste which made it a favorite amongst those that worked in the wild.

This one was young male and alone which was unusual. Norby's team was training outside the sensor line when the bera attacked. A creature this size would have set off the sensors, and it was nearly a week before the Foresters decided this one was just a stray.

The Foresters removed the claws from the bera and made necklaces for the Marines. The hide was stretched and tanned then given to Norby as a reminder of his time on Bellus.

Michael's Grand-Father's ship, the Petronius, entered orbit a day ahead of schedule. Since they arrived later in the evening, Michael advised them they would come up and see them the next morning. That night he could tell that Kaya was nervous about leaving the planet and meeting Michael's parents.

He decided to take Sergeant Norby with them, so his Grand-Father's personal physician could check on how his wounds were healing and take advantage of the ship's canteen for things the men needed. Michael knew that the Petronius was well stocked with about anything a person could desire.

As soon as the cargo hold was secure, and the atmosphere was Earth normal, Michael dropped the rear ramp to find an honor guard awaiting them with his parents and grandparents at the end of the double rows of Free Lancer's in their dress uniforms.

Kaya was in her crimson smock and silver slacks with Michael in a clean uniform without his equipment. As soon as Kaya stepped off the ramp, three distinct ringing of bells could be heard, then a voice making an announcement.

"The Throne of Bellus." Was all the announcement said.

Michael offered his arm which she took, and they walked between the Lancers who were at present arms. He could feel Kaya slightly trembling as they walked to meet his family. Michael stopped three paces short of his family.

"Mother, Father, Honored Grandparents, may I introduce Princess Kaya Swansea Denoyelles, The Throne of Bellus, and my wife."

Michael's mother stepped forward and offered both her hands to Kaya who took them.

"Michael, she is beautiful. The saints have blessed you. Kaya, welcome to our humble family, and we hope that you find great happiness with us."

"Thank you Mother Denoyelles. May I say that you have a wonderful son in Michael."

"You may Kaya but remember, we have known him longer than you, and know what a handful he can be."

Kaya laughed then Michael's mother leaned in, kissed her on the cheek then pulled her to introduce her to the rest of the family. Kaya was amazed at the appearance of Ireesha Denoyelles and her fur covered body. But the one thing that helped her through the process of meeting Michael's family was the feeling each of them towards her. Each of them were emitting a feeling of love for Michael and his bride. Kaya finally relaxed as they walked through the ship to a conference room, so they could speak in private.

Inside the conference room they found that there were two parts to it. One was the large, dark wood conference table made from wood only found on the planet named after its founder, Denoyelles. The second aspect was a sitting area of comfortable chairs and sofas set in a circular pattern with a small, knee high table in the middle which was covered with carafes of coffee and hot tea along with pitchers of various fruit juices. There were also plates of pastries and other items to snack on as they talked.

Michael got right down to business as the door to the room was closed and locked, so they would not be disturbed.

"Grand-Father, is this room being recorded?"

"Yes Michael, but only myself and your Grand-Mother can access those recordings. Is there some concern over what will be said in here?"

"Yes, there is, but that will also come out in time."

Michael and Kaya took a place on a small sofa while his Grand-Father took a padded chair across from them with Michael's Father sitting next to him with the women taking other chairs. But it was Grand-Mother Ireesha who made the first comment upon sitting.

"Kaya my dear, I feel that you are hiding something, and it is making you nervous. We are family here, and you have no need to hide anything from us."

Kaya smiled and felt Michael give her hand a gentle squeeze.

"Grand-Mother, do you feel my apprehension, or sense it?"

"Now that's an odd question Kaya. But we Centaurians have always been noted for being able to sense, if you will, if a person is lying, or telling the truth during conversations. It is one reason we are sought after as intelligence officers in both the Free Lancers and the Fleet."

"There is a reason for having that sense which you have Grand-Mother. You see it is genetic to your race and mine. If you compare your genetic profile, or what Michael calls DNA to mine, you will find that you and I are closer related to each other than we are to the rest of humanity. We both carry markers that belong to the Masters, the people who removed our ancestors from Earth. Your ancestors were taken to a planet we know as Zyra, while mine were brought here to Bellus."

No one spoke as each were trying to dissect what Kaya had just told them. She continued after a moment.

"Grand-Mother, at this moment you are thinking that if what I said was true, that would explain much about the irregularities in your DNA. And just moments before I spoke, Mother Denoyelles was thinking about how Michael's and my children would look, and if the silver hair was hereditary. Yes, Mother Denoyelles, it is hereditary and is only found within the ruling line of Bellus. It is in a sense our crown."

"Kaya, how could you know what I was thinking?" Michael's mother asked.

99

"Mother Denoyelles, the same way that Grand-Father Denoyelles is thinking that if I can read another's mind, then this is a very good reason to quarantine Bellus. Am I right Grand-Father?"

"Yes Kaya, that was exactly what I was thinking. Is this ability yours alone, or can others on Bellus do that?"

"Grand-Father, I must apologize in that it is a violation of Bellus Law to intrude into another's mind, but I felt that I needed to establish a valid reason for the quarantine, beyond the Federation Law concerning newly discovered races which Michael has explained to me."

Michael took over at this point and explained what he had discovered and the reasoning behind his quarantining the planet. He never spoke of the technology that the Bellusarians had available to them figuring on advising them of that later. Kaya had poured herself a cup of hot tea while he was talking. When he finished she poured him a cup and handed it to him then addressed Grand-Mother Ireesha.

"Yes Grand-Mother, I do like the tea, thank you. But there is another problem which Michael did not address. Our population is in decline due to the lack of genetic diversity. We hope that the children that Michael and I produce will help infuse enough diversity into my people, so we may survive as a race."

"Kaya, are you with child?" Michael's father asked.

"Yes, Father Denoyelles, I am."

This caught Michael off guard.

"Kaya, are you sure?" Michael asked.

"Yes, my love I am. I was examined when I returned to the capital and confirmed. Forgive me for not telling you Michael, but I know of your concern for my health, and did not wish to add to the problems you have been facing."

"Kaya, it is my place to worry about you. Never do this again, I am your husband and I should know about anything that affects you as this child will."

"What are the two of you talking about Michael?" Mother Denoyelles inquired.

"Mother, the problem with the decline in population on Bellus is due to the inability for the females to carry to term, and there is also a high risk to the mother."

Grand-Mother Ireesha stood as did Michael's mother.

"Come Kaya, we are going to take you to our personal physician, Doctor Vanova, so he can give you a physical, and maybe help find a way to make your pregnancy easier for you. He is an Altairian and they are very good at genetic problems."

After the women left for the medical compartment, Michael just sat back and enjoyed the tea that Kaya had given him. He was tempted to look into his Grand-Father's mind, but closed his mind to everything except for the link he held with Kaya. With the women out of the room Michael decided to give his Father and Grand-Father a demonstration of the technology the Bellusarians had available to them. Michael was wearing a personal cloaking device he had borrowed from one of the Foresters.

Michael stood and walked over to the door and stopped mid-way between the sitting area and the door. He stood with his hand on his hip as if just resting and spoke before he keyed the cloak control.

"Father, Grand-Father, here is another reason for quarantining Bellus."

Michael keyed the control and vanished, he then moved near the conference table and turned the cloak off. The look on his male ancestors was one of bewilderment.

"Son, how did you do that?" His father asked.

Michael keyed it again and moved across the room behind them and spoke while still cloaked.

"It is because of knowledge the Bellusarians have which comes from the alien race that kidnapped them."

His Grand-Father swiveled in his seat to look in the direction the voice came from.

"Michael, stop with these games and sit, we need to discuss this new development."

Michael walked to the sofa, and turned off the cloak before sitting.

"Kaya and I discussed this for a long time on whether to make this technology known to you. There are several things which I am aware of that must never find itself off the planet, and in the hands of people who could create massive harm to the peace of the universe."

"Can you tell us more Michael?" His father asked.

"Dad, you are half Centaurian where I am only a quarter, but I have discovered that I also have the same psychic abilities as Kaya. This can only mean you and Grand-Mother also have that ability but is buried deep in your mind. Mine was opened when Kaya and I touched as she was searching for a way for us to communicate. Their language is so very different than ours. When she touched my hand, we exchanged language knowledge, and in doing so she inadvertently unlocked my mind. Believe me it is not a gift I relish having."

"So, you can read our minds?"

"Yes Grand-Father I could if I wanted to, but I have closed my mind to everyone but Kaya. It has taken me weeks to learn how to do even that. But can you imagine what would happen if Uncle Abraham discovered this trait in himself?"

"Oh, saints no! He is dangerous enough as it is, but to read, maybe even control the minds of others would be like giving a child an armed fusion device and a hammer."

"Sir, the transference between myself and Kaya occurred because she desired the knowledge of my language, so we could communicate. The opening of my mind was an unexpected side effect. It was an accident, but one we cannot risk occurring again, especially with a full-blooded Centaurian such as Abraham."

"Son, how is it that the Centaurians and the Bellusarians have this ability while the rest of humanity does not?" His father asked.

"Dad, from what I have learned it is because the Masters, those that kidnapped both races, also had this trait, and it is embedded within the genetic markers found in both races when they were being experimented on, so the Masters race could survive its own demise. Also, the major difference between the races is that when the Masters abandoned Centaurians, they destroyed everything they built and left the people to survive on their own in the wild. It is suspected they did this as part of the experiment, but never returned to see its result."

Michael paused to first pour a fresh cup of tea, then took a sip to check how warm it was before continuing.

"When the Masters left Bellus, they left all of their labs intact along with the knowledge of how to utilize them. Somewhere out in the depths of uncharted space is the home planet of these Masters."

"Why haven't the Bellusarians ventured out into space?" His Grand-Father asked.

"Sir, it seems that the Masters warned them not to. The history of Bellus is one of confusion in those early years, and their mental abilities finally forced them to enact and enforce laws concerning the use of the psychic abilities which made them understand that they would be at risk if they moved out to rejoin humanity. Then they were also able to monitor much of humanities

103

conversations as they bled over into this part of space. We space born humans frightened them."

"Why do they desire contact now?" His father inquired.

Michael explained about the problems with the decline in population and the corruption of their DNA. He held nothing back concerning Kaya's mission to bring fresh DNA diversity into the race even at the cost of her own life. Michael even told of how he fell in love with her and she with him. He left nothing out as he spoke about her and the world below them.

"So, Michael, I take it you are hoping the Altairians can cure Kaya as they did my mother Jilena?" His Grand-Father asked.

"Yes Grand-Father, I pray to the saints that they can help her, because even though we have been together for such a short time, I cannot fathom life without her now."

The conversation turned to other matters as they waited for the women to return from Kaya's visit to the doctor. When the women returned Michael was handed good and bad news.

Kaya was still in good health as was the fetus developing within her. She had explained the problems of her people in carrying to term and the risk of death the mother could face. Doctor Vanova had ran a quick analysis of her DNA and compared it to records on file referencing normal humans with similar problems. Jilena Denoyelles' records were in that file and her own condition gave hope that a cure could be found.

The bad news was Doctor Vanova wanted to send Kaya to Altair for treatment. The only other choice was to bring a research team to Bellus, and do the work in a medical research ship in orbit. Either way it was a four-month trip, and that did not consider getting a vessel to Bellus to take her to Altair, or that the only ship the Altairian's had capable of this kind of research was available.

Michael's Grand-Father proposed another idea. To use the orbiting Frigate to transport Kaya to Altair. It was faster than the ships otherwise which would carry her, and she would be under the care of the Altairian physician aboard that vessel. Kaya said she would have to talk with the Council before any decision of this nature could be made.

There was a concern that without the Frigate in orbit, Abraham would risk going to the surface to further his research. Ireesha told Michael that as long as she was in orbit, Abraham would not dare risk leaving the security of his ship and going to the surface. But Michael could not accompany Kaya to Altair since he had placed the quarantine on the planet, he had to stay on the planet to insure the quarantine stayed in place.

Then there was the fact that Michael's Grand-Father had to go before the Federation Congress with his credentials to insure the quarantine was fixed and guaranteed by the Federation before diplomatic relations could begin. Another ship could come from Hanover to return him to stand before Congress, but that would also take two months.

It was time that was the enemy, but one that could be defeated with proper planning. Being the Duke Denoyelles had its perks as Michael's Grand-Father called for another vessel to return him to Hanover and the Federation Congress. He then arranged for the Frigate Rostislav to be placed at the disposal of the Princess of Bellus for transport to Altair for medical treatment, when arrangements could be made with the Bellus Council.

Michael and Kaya ate the mid-day meal aboard the ship before gathering Sergeant Norby up and returning to the surface. Norby had several containers loaded with comfort items for both the Marines and the Foresters. He had also left the wound treatment cream the Foresters had used on his wounds with Doctor Vanova to test, since his wounds were healing at a much faster rate than normal.

Ireesha told Michael to have no further contact with Abraham until they could all meet face to face after Kaya had a chance to confer with the Council concerning her going to Altair for treatment.

A party was held at the campsite that evening as Norby presented the Foresters with things they had never seen before such as chocolates and sweet meats. He had also brought several bottles of wine from Aurora which Michael agreed to their rationing during this party. Everyone had a good time and Kaya admitted she enjoyed the smaller portion of wine she drank since she was with child. Tomorrow her and Michael would go to face the Council with the news of her pregnancy and the offer of medical treatment.

Prince Michael

A multi-passenger cloak capable vessel came for Kaya and Michael to take the to the Capital to meet with the Council. They were met at the Cathedral's landing pad by Titus who told them the craft would be loaded with supplies for the Foresters at the camp site, and that Kaya could fly it back and keep it there for resupply, or other missions requiring larger than a single craft such as the Foresters had at hand.

The meeting this day was held in the private conference room of the Council. It had a single, large table with chairs around it for the members. There was a chair for Michael since he was now considered Prince of Bellus, but he chose to stand to Kaya's left as the meeting was being held. Jiazi was present as per Kaya's request and sat to Kaya's right for this meeting.

The meeting started with Kaya briefing the Council on her actions concerning the Duke Denoyelles' acceptance of the position as representative of Bellus to the Federation Council and Congress. Michael had to explain the design of the Federation and their influence throughout the universe.

There was some dissention at first by members of the Council, but Michael stepped in to once more explain how he had contacted his family to insure he was following the legal form when he placed Bellus under quarantine to prevent the Centaurians from landing, and possibly discovering their latent psychic abilities. Kaya reminded the Council of the Masters warnings concerning contact with off-worlders.

The Council was aware that Kaya had gone with Michael to meet with his Grand-Father on his ship, but was not aware of what followed.

Kaya announced she was with child and had been examined by a doctor who felt his people could help correct the genetic problems the Bellusarian females had with childbirth. Michael once more stepped in and explained how the Altairian people specialized in medical and the science of genetics. He told of his own Great-

Grandmother's problems, and how they had been corrected which mean she was able to give birth to his own Grandfather years later. When he was challenged on the ability of the Altairian scientist's verses Bellusarian scientists, Michael explained that the Altairian's had been working in genetics for over two hundred standard years, and with over one hundred different races where the Bellusarians had only recently became interested in genetics.

The Council conceded that Kaya's best chances to deliver a child, and to survive the experience was in the hands of the Altairian's, but were concerned about her being gone, away from the throne for such a long time. Kaya agreed that it was also her concern, but she had only been on the throne for a short time and the Council had governed for years before that. With Jiazi acting as her Chancellor, she felt the Council would continue to serve the people as before while she was gone.

Michael was asked what his position would be in relation to the Council since he could not leave as long as the quarantine was in effect. His response was clear to them that he was Prince in name only, and that since he was not familiar with the culture and customs of Bellus, he would abstain from setting on the throne while Kaya was gone, and deferred to Jiazi to act for the throne.

He was asked if he would act in a ceremonial fashion when needed to stand as the throne of Bellus. Michael's reply was only if he received the customs guidelines in enough time to study and practice them, so he would not make a mockery of the throne. But he would only act as the ceremonial face of the throne, not the legal face. His explanation was accepted by the Council.

Kaya advised that as soon as arrangements could be made, she was leaving for Altair, and that once the days meeting was concluded, Jiazi was to assume the face of the throne for all functions except where Michael was called for. She asked each Council person for their vote of confidence for Jiazi and received each vote as an affirmative in support. Kaya concluded the meeting, then retired to her apartment to pack for the trip.

A Harsh Discovery

The Denoyelles men were sitting around the conference table with their wives awaiting the arrival of the one man none of them wished to see, but knew they had to appear to make the effort. Abraham Kerekes had been messaging both the Duke and Michael daily demanding an audience. Kaya was to depart for Altair once the meeting was over, and everyone was wanting to see her off for her own safety.

Abraham was already upset when he arrived on the Petronius instead of them coming to him, but when the Lancer Captain refused to allow his aides to accompany him into the conference room, he became very vocal in what he felt was unjust treatment at the hands of a furless creature. Captain Mendoza was polite and informed him that either he entered alone, or he could be escorted back to his shuttle and return to his own ship. What Mendoza never said was that his mother was also a Centaurian, and he felt the insult to his father was uncalled for. Abraham entered the conference room alone.

In the conference room, he found himself sitting in the middle of the table with the Duke at one end, and Kaya at the other. Michael was sitting to Kaya's right, so he had direct line of sight on Abraham. Abraham had an empty seat on either side of him with his sister in position to look directly at him. Michael could feel Abraham's anger building inside of him, and Kaya squeezed Michael's hand as if to tell him to relax, she had things under control if need be.

Abraham immediately wanted to know why his research teams were not allowed on the planet. The Duke acting as representative of Bellus gave him a doctored reason based on Federation Law. The Duke, then repeated that the only people who could revoke the quarantine were Michael, or the Head of State for Bellus, the Princess Kaya, Michael's wife.

Michael felt a weak touch to his mind as Abraham gave them a glowering look. Kaya touched his mind telling him that Abraham had discovered the latent talent of mental control, but was untrained and weak of talent. Abraham was trying to influence Michael and Kaya to cancel the quarantine. Kaya entered the conversation at this point.

"Uncle Abraham, if I may call you that, what is the real reason for wanting on the surface of Bellus?"

Abraham knew with his sister sitting across from him he had no choice, but to accept being called Uncle Abraham by this alien female. Michael and Kaya could feel the hatred building inside him.

"We believe there is a cure for our affliction caused by the monsters that kidnapped our ancestors and experimented on them, causing the Centaurian people to look like animals from a horror vid."

"On the contrary Uncle Abraham, I believe the Centaurian people are beautiful. Your sister is a prime example of that beauty. And my father-in-law is handsome with his rich, black fur. No Abraham, I believe you have a more sinister reason for searching Bellus. What is that reason?"

Kaya and Michael could feel Abraham trying to enter their minds, but both were able to block him without trouble. For weeks Kaya had been training Michael, so he could control the strength of his mind, and in doing so he found blocking someone like Abraham simple.

"I have stated my purpose so why are you trying to make it seem I am lying to you?"

Kaya uncovered a crystal cube she had earlier placed on the table and covered with a cloth napkin. She ran her hand over it and the figured that appeared was a Centaurian. She smiled at Abraham then once again spoke.

"Uncle Abraham, the figure you see from the crystal is not a Centaurian, but one of the Masters, the people who kidnapped your people and mine. We know much about them, about what they did to your people. Abraham, your fur is not from a failed experiment, so much as it is from the Masters breeding with your females. Over several generations, only those with fur survived and the genetic

110

material transferred to the children of your race carried forward. Our scientists think that if your people breed with Earth normal humans only, then after several generations, the adaptive fur would all but disappear from your race. But as I said, I believe you have another reason, a more sinister reason for wanting to find the laboratories the Masters left behind."

Abraham all but jumped up from his chair.

"I will not be spoken to in this manner!"

He suddenly found himself being slamming back onto his chair, unable to move except for his head as he looked at Kaya. He tried to speak, but was unable to utter a word as he began to drool. Kaya stood and walked around the table to Abraham with every eye on her as no one spoke. She placed her hand on his forehead then laughed.

"Abraham, you are a fool. You discovered your talent, but it is weak compared to Michael's ability. You were hoping to find a way to make your abilities stronger, so you could seek revenge on those who you think slight you for your appearance. You are a weak man Abraham, that is why the woman you loved found another, not because of the way you look. I can see her as clear as day in your mind telling you what I just told you, but you could never accept her truth. Now I shall give you another truth, you will go down to Bellus and you will enter the Chamber. When you are removed from that demonic creation of the Masters, you will be stripped of any psychic abilities, even the ability to judge if a person is lying or telling the truth."

Kaya removed her hand from his forehead and he collapsed in the chair, then slowly slid off onto the floor.

"Michael, we need to get him to the Capital as quick as possible. Take him down and turn him over to the Foresters, and tell them to get him to Titus immediately. I'll contact Titus and advise him of Abraham's condition and Titus will do the rest. Hurry, I have no idea how long Abraham will be unconscious."

111

Kaya took a step towards her chair and stumbled. Michael caught her before she fell.

"Kaya, are you alright?"

"I'll be fine my love, but such contact between people is trying, and I had to go deeper into his mind that I have every gone before even with you. He is a sick man, believing he can find revenge in such a manner."

Duke Denoyelles pushed a button on the table and Captain Mendoza immediately entered the room.

"Captain Mendoza, take Doctor Kerekes to Baron Denoyelles shuttle immediately, and take two men with you to watch Doctor Kerekes until the Baron can turn him over to the people on the ground."

"Yes Sir." Mendoza called for two of his men in the hall who entered and followed Mendoza's instructions in removing Abraham from the conference room.

Michael helped Kaya to her chair, kissed her on her forehead and left to take Abraham to the surface. Grand-Mother Ireesha shifted some, then spoke to Kaya.

"Kaya, is that truly a holograph of who you call the Masters?"

"Yes, Grand-Mother, it is. The only information they did not leave when they departed was the location of their home world."

"That information destroys centuries of speculation about how the Centaurians came to be. Now what about Abraham?"

"Be at peace Grand-Mother. When he returns he will still have his intelligence, his knowledge and will be at peace with his past. Also, the psychic ability that he was trying to nurture will have been carefully removed. For a Bellusarian, the loss of our mental abilities is like losing an arm or leg."

"Daughter, what do you need to contact your people about Abraham?" Michael's father inquired.

Kaya tapped the side of her head.

"I have already done so Father, they are preparing for his arrival as we speak. Forgive me, but I am tired."

Michael's father went to her, picked her up from her chair and took her to one of the sofas across the room and laid her down on it.

"Rest Daughter, Michael will return as soon as he can, so he can see you off on your journey."

Kaya just closed her eyes and fell asleep almost immediately.

As Kaya slept, the Duke went to the detachment of Lancers who provided security for his person and the Duchess. In this detachment were a platoon of female Lancers who were concerned with the Duchess's safety. He instructed Senior Lieutenant Alecia Bascalo to select eight of her detail to go with Kaya to Altair and insure her safety. Considering her medical situation, Bascalo selected four female medics as part of the detail to insure a medic was always on hand. Bascalo was to accompany Kaya acting as Kaya's Lady in Waiting to insure there were no difficulties with the Fleet or on Altair during this assignment.

The detail drew civilian clothing from the ships stores more in tune with being the entourage of royalty to hide their function. This was something the Duchess Ireesha never required since she was a Lancer when she met the Duke, and the entire universe knew that the Lancers provided security for the entire Denoyelles family when traveling from Hanover.

It was nearly four hours before Michael returned to be with Kaya. He found her still on the sofa asleep where his father had placed her. His mother was sitting nearby in a chair watching over her while the others had left the room to deal with other family business. Michael gently woke her with a kiss to her lips.

"Time to get up honey. We need to get you over to the Rostislav, so you can be on your way to Altair."

"I know Michael, I was just so tired after dealing with Abraham."

Michael helped her off the sofa and to their shipboard quarters. She checked her bags to insure she had what she needed and that she was not taking anything which might disclosed the secrets Michael was working hard at keeping away from the rest of the universe.

Two Lancers followed Michael and Kaya as they carried her luggage to the shuttle. The Denoyelles family was waiting for them when they entered the bay. The Duke introduced Kaya to her security detail before the detail boarded the shuttle. Each of the family kissed Kaya on her cheek and wished her a pleasant journey. The Duke had prepared papers for her to sign as per an earlier conversation, and she read to insure they said what she felt needed before the Duke went before the Bellus Council to talk with them before he went to the Federation Congress.

Kaya was greeted by the Captain and officers of the Rostislav along with an Honor Guard of Marines when she exited the shuttle. She was the Head of State for an entire world and the Fleet was going to treat her as such. The Captain had surrendered his own quarters for her to use during this voyage.

Michael gave her one last kiss before he left her quarters. Neither wanted to be separated in such a manner, but understood that it had to be done this way to protect Bellus from intrusion by outsiders now that it was slowly being made aware of its existence by the rest of the universe.

Just as the Rostislav boosted from orbit Michael felt Kaya's touch and her love for him. He returned her feelings and locked her emotions into his own psychic to have them while she was gone. He sat in his quarters aboard his Grand-Father's ship and fought the urge to curl up from the empty feeling that was inside of him. Michael never considered the psychic touch of Kaya would have such a hold on him.

The Bellus Council

Duke Denoyelles stood before the Bellus Council in the private meeting chambers to present his credentials with Michael by his side.

"Honored Council of Bellus, I am Duke Jeremy Denoyelles, Grand-Father of Baron Michael Denoyelles. I understand that through the efforts of Princess Kaya Denoyelles, the Council understands what we call Fed Speak, and can read its writings. I present to you the document signed by Princess Kaya prior to her departure for Altair for your consideration."

He moved to the conference table and gently laid it on the table since he was unsure of whom to give it to. It was picked up and passed down to Jiazi who opened it and read the single page inside the folder. She then passed it to her right for the next person to read before speaking.

"Duke Denoyelles, as Chancellor to the Throne of Bellus, I welcome you to our world. Please take a seat at our humble table. Prince Michael, please take the seat normally reserved for the Princess as is custom."

"Chancellor Jiazi, I shall take the seat next to my wife's as no person shall sit in her place. My title is appreciated, but I am not qualified to sit in such an exalted place." Michael responded.

Jiazi gave a light laugh then smiled at Michael.

"Michael, Kaya's father hated that seat and I am certain he and you would have been grand friends. Please take whichever seat suits you. Now as soon as each member has a chance to read the document the Princess signed for Bellus, we shall discuss what is necessary to protect and preserve Bellus."

The meeting lasted for over two hours as each member of the Council gave their thoughts on the mission Duke Denoyelles was to take on their behalf. Duke Denoyelles spent a lot of time explaining how the Federation conducted business as Council members brought up points they felt needed covered. Once a program was laid out which the Council could approve, the Duke was shown quarters in the Cathedral near Kaya's apartment where Michael would stay while at the Capital. Michael hated to be in Kaya's apartment because it reminded him of her departure from his life.

Kaya was learning the names of her entourage and educating them at the same time on the public conduct of what the Fleet were referring to as Hand Maids. In private, the atmosphere was less formal with the female Lancers teaching Kaya games to help pass the time. She had to close her mind during the card games, so she would not know what the other players had in their hands.

If Kaya had taken a regular ship to Altair from Bellus the journey would have taken three days beyond four months. But a Fleet Frigate was capable of faster speeds and it was calculated the time to achieve orbit around Altair was reduced by just over two weeks. The Lancer medics took Kaya's vital signs daily along with several non-intrusive tests as instructed by Doctor Vanova before they left Bellus, so they would have as much information for the Doctors on Altair as possible upon arrival.

Four days after Kaya departed for Altair, Michael collected Abraham from the Bellusarians. He did not take him directly to the Institute ship, but to see his sister, Ireesha. Ireesha later told Michael that Abraham was more like he was in their youth. Once again Abraham was thoughtful of others and almost meek. Whomever the female was that broke his heart, had created a monster compared to the man who was buried inside him by hate.

Soon after Abraham returned to his own ship, they boosted from orbit to return to Hawking's World to wait for the day that Bellus would become a member of the Federation, and eventually open to visiting scientists.

The Duke departed two weeks later, on a fast courier for Hanover leaving his ship in orbit. From an untrained eye, The Petronius looked like a large, commercial space vessel, but to anyone who had served in the Fleet could see it was larger and better armed and armored than a Fleet Heavy Cruiser.

The Federation

Duke Denoyelles presented his credentials to the Federation Council, then requested a meeting of the Federation Congress to address the recognition of Bellus as a sovereign world. He stood before the Congress not in his livery of the Denoyelles but in a suit, he would wear for a business meeting.

"Members of the Federation Congress, I address you today not as Duke Denoyelles, but as Jeremy Denoyelles, Special Envoy for the Bellusarian Government. For those not completely aware, Bellus is a newly discovered planet just outside the Southern Rim of charted space."

"The world has a hereditary Princess who currently sits on the throne, along with a ruling Council of twelve, who were selected by the people of Bellus to govern them. As many here know my Grandson, Baron Michael Denoyelles has been on the planet for several months surveying it upon request of the Hawking's Institute and the Fleet. What he has discovered required him to issue a quarantine under Article Nine of the Discovered Species Act placed into Federation Law by my father, the Count Denoyelles."

"Her Royal Highness Princess Kaya Swansea is not a ruler in your typical form, but worked out in the wilderness of the planet as what the Bellusarians call a Forester, which in the Federation is a Conservationist. Fate placed Baron Denoyelles in her path, and they met while he was surveying the ruins of an ancient city for the Hawking's Institute."

"Here I must make the Federation aware of the fact that the Bellusarian people are the results of humans being kidnapped by aliens and taken to this planet as were the Centaurians. It has been established that the Bellusarians and the Centaurians are genetically related due to the aliens which the Bellusarians refer to as The Masters."

"Now the difference between the Centaurians and the Bellusarians is that the Centaurians are the result of interbreeding between the kidnapped humans and the Masters, whereas the

117

Bellusarians were only used in genetic research. Also, when the Masters left Hawking's World which is known to the Bellusarians as Zyra, they destroyed all their labs and cities before leaving the planet. On Bellus, they left the key laboratories intact along with the knowledge of how to use them."

"It was the discovery of the knowledge of the Masters and their laboratories that caused Baron Denoyelles to place a quarantine on the planet. The discovery of the Centaurians nearly destroyed their race which was the basis for the Discovered Species Act."

"Baron Denoyelles contacted me with the consent of the Princess Kaya to act as a representative of Bellus to the Federation Congress. It is the desire of the Council of Bellus, with the approval of the Princess, that Bellus remain under quarantine until a complete analysis can be made of the technology available to them, concerning the effect it could have upon the member planets of the Federation."

"One final note to all of this is that the Princess Kaya and the Baron Denoyelles have married which has elevated him to the title Prince Michael of Bellus. This marriage occurred after he placed Bellus under quarantine. Also, he has declined to accept any royal position or authority granted by the Council of Bellus."

"Members of the Federation. Baron Michael Denoyelles is also a serving Fleet Marine Officer with the rank of Captain. He has been decorated for gallantry three times and wears two wound stripes on his uniform. He has recognized that some of the alien technology he has discovered on Bellus could be misused if it falls into the wrong hands, and upon being made aware of several aspects of their technology, I must agree with his assessment."

"I see a few scornful faces on members of Congress, but as Duke Denoyelles, I hereby swear before this gathering that the Denoyelles family will not profit from a single piece of technology found on Bellus, unless the entire Federation profits the same. As the Federation knows, the word of a Denoyelles is their bond and has never been broken."

118

"It is hereby requested by the Council of Bellus with the approval of the Princess Kaya that the Federation passes a resolution of quarantine on the Bellus planet until they can evaluate which technology they can make public or which they will keep concealed due to the risk of harm to the Federation."

"All pertinent information is available within the resolution packet presented to the President of the Federation. I thank you for your time."

Four hours later the resolution passed with a ninety-seven percent approval of the members of Congress. An hour later seven Federation warships boosted towards Bellus to establish a buffer between Bellus and known space. The only exceptions to passage to Bellus was the Denoyelles family, who were to function as advisors and envoys between Bellus and the Federation.

Slowly the word leaked out that Kaya was enroute to Altair due to a medical condition. It was made known by the Fleet that any attempt to interfere with the Princess Kaya would result in swift action by the Fleet, since she was under their protection even once she reached Altair.

Kaya received the notice of the resolution enroute to Altair through Fleet channels. She communicated as often as she could with Michael using a back channel the Marines normally used for operational data.

Seven weeks into the journey, Kaya began to become ill after eating and could not keep food down. The ship's cook did everything he could to provide her with something she could keep on her stomach to provide nourishment for her and the child she was carrying. By the ninth week, the ship's doctor had her on intravenous feeding as she was becoming weak.

They were able to vid-chat for the last time when she was three weeks from Altair. From her appearance, it appeared she had lost nearly a quarter of her weight and was weak. She was pleased to tell Michael she was carrying a son and he was in good health, even if she wasn't. They exchanged words of love before she had to break the connection because of her weakness.

119

Waiting

For Michael, waiting was becoming a burden that he was unsure of being able to deal with. He no longer had anything to do other than to walk Bellus without a goal in sight. Even though he at first forbid it, two security teams were always with him away from the camp. As the Foresters explained, the area they were in was part of the migratory route of the bera this time of the year, and it was noticed that he was always in thought as he walked, and was never really aware of his surroundings.

The Rostislav was a week out from Altair when Michael received a message from the Rostislav's doctor that Kaya was in a coma and on life support. The baby seemed unaffected by her condition and was well within normal perimeters of its growth.

Michael flew to the Capital which had dropped its cloak as the universe knew about them now to see Jiazi. His mother-in-law was already aware of Kaya's condition and she just held Michael as they sat in her quarters as he finally broke down. He blamed himself for her condition, even as he accepted she would have done what she did with any man to hopefully save her people.

He knew he could not stay in Kaya's apartment, so he returned to the camp and searched for something to do. The Marines had trained the Foresters as well as possible without playing war games and such, so there was nothing for him to do there until Titus came to his camp.

Bellus had never had what could be called a police force because of the nature of the people. The Foresters were as close to a military organization as anything on the planet, but with Bellus moving into the universe of humanity, there was a rising concern of eventually people coming and creating problems best handled without the massive use of psychic powers.

Michael called the Marines in to get their input on training a group of one hundred Foresters in the manner of Marines. Sergeant McKenzie stated that the Foresters were quick learners and absorbed the information quickly. Sergeant Norby echoed that comment and added they were very proficient with modern firearms.

Titus told them that since the Council had approved this action, that the Marines who had been working with the Foresters were being granted the title of Citizens of Bellus, and that they would also be the nucleus of the Bellusarian Security Force (BSF) with Prince Denoyelles as commander.

Michael laughed as he then told McKenzie, he was now a Senior Lieutenant in the BSF and Norby was a Lieutenant. Sergeant Paxton was now a Gunnery Sergeant and the other two Marines were Senior Sergeants. Michael would maintain his rank as Captain and Titus would be the commander.

When Titus announced he would also go through the training, McKenzie spoke up before Michael could.

"Lord Titus, you need to understand that you will not be treated any different than the others. You will eat what they eat, sleep where they sleep, and be treated as they will be treated during the training. Baron Denoyelles was not exempt when he joined the Marines, nor should you be."

"Senior Lieutenant McKenzie, the Council has determined that eventually all Foresters will be trained in such a fashion, and as being the head of the Foresters, how can I lead them if I do not know how they are trained, or what they are capable of accomplishing."

"As long as we have an understanding Lord Titus."

Michael smiled at the way McKenzie handled what could have been a touchy subject later during training. During the meeting, it was determined that the female Foresters already on the scene would become his clerks while the men remained as security personal.

They would also have to move to another location which could provide a substantial water source to handle the number of personal involved, plus have enough fairly level terrain for rifle ranges.

Michael quickly made up a short list of items which the Council would have to present to Duke Denoyelles to arrange transfer from the Fleet to the Bellus Government. This list included weapons, equipment vests with all necessary items for recruit level training and helmets. Bellus had the capability to produce the uniforms and other items they would need as training progressed.

The message of Kaya entering the Altairian Genetic Institute lightened Michael's heart knowing she was now in the care of the best genetic scientists in the universe. Four days later he received another message that the fetus, his son, had been removed from Kaya and placed in an artificial womb and was in good health. Kaya was still in a coma and on life support, but was stable. All he could do was hope this action would save his beloved Kaya.

All Michael could do now was develop a training program for the Foresters as he waited further news of his son and Kaya.

Training the Militia

To the Universe, the only thing worse than having Fleet Marines drop in to quell a revolt was having the Free Lance Infantry show up on your doorstep in the middle of the night. What most of the universe did not know was that a vast majority of Lancers were in fact former Marines, who were now working at their trade as mercenaries.

One aspect no one seemed to notice was that Marines did their own engineering, construction of bases and such when the Fleet's Engineers were busy elsewhere. This was the first thing on the list of accomplishments to be made once the trainees, or recruits were on the ground. Sergeant, now Lieutenant McKenzie submitted a list of equipment that most Fleet vessels carried to support their Marines and their own operations.

Soon the new area selected was covered with stacks of cases and crates containing everything from carbines, pistols, ammunition, hammers, and nails. The blockade ships in orbit were fixed in the duty of guarding Bellus and they cleaned out their holds to support the operation on the planet.

As one Heavy Destroyer Commander put it: "The costs in material and the expense of down shipping those items to the Marines already on the surface who need those things to train the locals, can be far cheaper than sending my Marines down and bringing body bags back up later."

Michael notified Titus that to insure each individual received the training necessary, there would need to be people available to prepare the meals for the trainees, so they would not have to concern themselves with that task or miss days of training while taking care of the others. Titus sent a message back the next day and asked if ten older Foresters, people they felt was too old to go through the training, would be sufficient to deal with such a detail. Michael told him ten were plenty, but if they found the need for more to have them standing ready.

The days were full of activity getting ready for the trainees, but the nights wore on Michael as he lay alone in the bed he had shared with Kaya and prayed to the saints for her wellbeing.

Michael arranged for a clerk to come down and teach his clerks the forms and records needed for each person they would be training. He first went into the system and modified the forms to read Bellusarian Security Force, then took each form and worked them to be applicable to the Bellusarians.

Two weeks after Titus had returned to the capital, the first transport load of trainees reported. The Bellusarian Security Detail mingled with the new people, transferring the knowledge of Fed Speak to each one. The new people had an advantage in that some of the jargon the original detail had to learn the hard way was transferred to them with the rest of the language.

Titus arrived with the last transport dressed as the rest and asked Michael if he could address them one time before training started. Michael approved, then moved away with his Marines to allow Titus to speak. It surprised Michael that Titus used Fed Speak instead of Bellusarian.

"Fellow Foresters, I stand before you not as the leader of the Foresters, nor as Lord Titus, but as Trainee Titus."

He took a badge off his uniform and held it high for all to see.

"This badge marks my position as a Forester just as many of you wear badges showing your positions. Here there is only Captain Denoyelles and his Marines who hold a position of importance."

Titus dropped his badge into the dirt.

"Remove your badges because the next time you place an emblem of authority upon your uniform, it will because Captain Denoyelles has judged you to receive it. The Council has even dictated my retaining my place within the Foresters, and the fledging Bellus Security Force on my being able to complete the training ahead of us."

"Also from this moment on, the only language to be spoken or heard within these training grounds is the language of our teachers. Even amongst yourselves in the dark of night, only speak the language of the Federation, so it will come as natural to you as our own language."

"One final note. Captain Denoyelles is also Prince Denoyelles, husband and mate to our precious Princess Kaya. It is his desire to only be known as Captain Denoyelles, and so it shall be. Good luck to each of you. I have said all I need to say, thank you."

As Titus began to walk to the crowd of Bellusarians waiting to see what was next, Michael winked at Gunny Paxton took the wink as a queue and his voice could be heard across the distance.

"Trainee Titus, did I see you drop something on my deck!"

Titus froze, then slowly turned back to see Paxton moving towards him.

"Excuse me Sergeant?"

"That's Gunny you meathead! Now did you drop trash on my deck or not?"

"I don't understand Gunny."

Paxton stopped where Titus had dropped his badge and stood over it. He pointed to the badge on the ground.

"Trainee Titus, any place I put my feet is a deck, making this is my deck. And what do I see at my feet, but a shiny trinket you dropped on my deck making my deck trashy. Do you know how to do a push up meathead?"

"No Gunny, I have no idea what a push up is?"

"I'll show you what a push up is, and you will follow what I do, so you can learn how to do a push up."

Paxton dropped to the ground and was in the front leaning rest position scowling at Titus. Titus went down on the ground and copied Paxton's position. Paxton began to lower himself to the ground, but stopped short of touching the ground. Titus went down, but continued until he had his chest on the ground. Paxton barked at him.

"Meathead, the only points of contact between you and my deck are your toes and hands! Get your belly off my deck!"

Paxton took Titus through five push-ups before he stood and told Titus to do five more, then stand and pick up his trash. He looked at the crowd of Foresters and saw several with grins on their faces. This was his second queue and he whistled loud which brought his junior Sergeants to him.

"So, some of you people think it was funny that Trainee Titus had to do push-ups, do you? Everyone down and give me ten push-ups. Now!"

For the next twenty minutes, the three Sergeants worked through the crown berating one for not doing the push-up properly then another for laughing and requiring ten more push-ups.

When Paxton felt they had enough he stood back from them and singled out one person and told them to come to him. He told him to stand perfectly still and extend his left arm out to his side. He called for another and positioned him an arm's length behind the first then told him to also extend his arm. Paxton then called for nine people to come and join on the first man, copying his arm extension and only moving close enough so the hand touched the shoulder. Once accomplished he brought nine more to fill in the second rank.

He continued this pattern until he had everyone in a twenty-person section with Titus being in the fourth section as the twenty-first man. Paxton explained this was now their family. When he gave the command fall-in, this was how they should look and before training was over they would look even better than they looked now.

Paxton numbered the sections one through five and told them that this was how they would eat, sleep, train, and anything else that required to be done. He told them that when he gave the command fall-out, everyone would go collect their personal belongings and return to their spot in the formation for further orders.

Once they had their baggage and packs and back in formation, Michael moved to them as Paxton stood and saluted with Michael returning the salute. Paxton moved aside, giving Michael unobstructed view of the formation.

"I am aware as Foresters you are used to working alone or in small groups. Here you will learn how to be a small part of a larger group. You will learn that a single mistake by a single individual can get others killed, or badly injured. The Gunny and his Sergeants will make you believe that the saints have forsaken you and placed you in the bowels of hell, but remember, facing another person in combat does not allow you to shirk the responsibility of the person to your left or right. The men and women in your squad are the most important people in the universe now. Without them you are nothing but meat to be ground up and fed to the beasts."

"At any time if you feel you cannot complete this training, report to my clerks who will arrange for your transportation back to the Capital. There is no sin in failing to complete our training. But the worst sin or crime any of you can commit is in failing to do your duty and causing another to suffer or die. To live knowing you failed those to your left or right is a burden you must never face because it is without a doubt, a fate worse than death itself."

"If you believe we are too harsh on you during training remember this, each of us Marines have endured worse. Yes, worse because we are only going to give you a taste of what we had to endure to become Marines. You have tonight to consider your fate, come tomorrow morning, we start training in earnest."

Michael looked at the faces of the people in front of him and could feel a mixture of feelings from them. He closed his mind from those feelings and called for Gunny Paxton. They exchanged salutes then Paxton took over the formation. Paxton moved the formation into the tree line and explained the until barracks could be built they would sleep in their individual tents they used as Foresters. They would pitch their tents where they were standing with a large gap between sections. Once their tents were erected, the anchor man or squad leader would come to the Instructors Assault Boat and retrieve rations for the evening meal. He reminded them that this was now their home and to keep it neat and tidy.

Later when one of the females asked about relieving her bowels, Sergeant Mueller gave her a shovel and took her off away from the tents and instructed her in digging a latrine. Others came and assisted, then when it was complete, they took turns using it and covering up the waste with a shovel or two of dirt.

No one reported for return to the Capital the next morning which did not surprise Michael. Physical training was conducted the next morning before they turned to building their camp. First would be a latrine system while at the same time a kitchen for hot meals. They had to cut down trees, moved them by hand to the saw mill that had been brought down for this purpose, then the lumber was cut and stacked to air dry before the building could be started.

Day after day the work grew harder as the Sergeants pushed them to get the buildings up so training could begin. What the Foresters never knew was they were learning the principals of engineering as they were building strength. During breaks the Sergeants would give them lectures on a variety of subjects that they would be covering later.

Soon they had the kitchen up with water running to it and a waste system out to a lagoon for waste water. Next came the barracks which were small for only twenty individuals in each one with modest sanitary facilities. No one move into the barracks until all of them were complete. Even their bunks had to be made from the wood they cut and sawed.

Next came the ranges. The trainees were broken into two groups of two sections each with one group constructing the pistol ranges, while the other worked building the rifle ranges. The fifth section handled the requirement for lumber or timbers. As this was happening, McKenzie looked for a location for an obstacle course. The terrain around the camp was relatively flat which was fine for a basic course, but Michael and McKenzie had other things on their minds.

A basic course was laid out extending three hundred meters from start to finish. The group constructing the pistol ranges finished first and turned to building the basic course, then were joined by the rifle range group.

When the basic course was complete, work was begun on the Master Course which started fifty meters from the end of the basic course. A large trench over two hundred meters long was dug then obstacles laid into it for the trainees to defeat as they moved down the trench. The trainees did not think it would be too difficult to deal with until they had to fill the trench with water, covering some obstacles or the obstacles just barely out of the water requiring the trainees to go under it to move to the next obstacle. What frightened most of the trainees was one obstacle in the middle of the trench.

In the middle of the trench, two-meter long plastron tubes were sunk just below the water which would require the trainee to crawl through the tube, under water, to move to the next obstacle. McKenzie explained that no one could ever predict what they might have to navigate as they moved to, or from an enemy position. This would also instill trust in their helmets ability to keep liquids or gases from choking them while providing them with a limited supply of oxygen.

From the trench, other obstacles had to be conquered such as a twenty-meter tall hill made of large boulders that were lifted from various locations around the planet by the grav-lift hooks on the assault boat. Ropes were strung on both sides to assist the climbers going up or down the hill.

Once the final nail was driven, training began hard, fast and nasty as the Foresters learned everything from basic rifle marksmanship to hand to hand combat. The Foresters beloved swords were left hanging over the head of their bunks as they learned how Marines fought.

The days became longer as training moved from the ranges into the forests and meadows around the camp. Injuries were dealt with on the spot and the salves the Foresters had was a miracle in healing a cut or abrasion that might require more treatment by a physician. One of the Doctor's from a Frigate in orbit volunteered to come to the surface and be available if needed. In two days, a six-bed clinic with sleeping quarters for the Doctor was built and ready for him to occupy.

Five weeks into training, Michael received notice that the baby was doing fine, and that Kaya was slowly gaining strength even though she was still in a coma. The Altairian scientists believed they had discovered the problem and were working to find a cure. Only time would tell.

For Michael, the fact the baby was developing, and Kaya was appearing to recover was all the news he needed to ease the anguish he fought nightly, and he was finally able to rest.

Eight weeks after forming up for training, the trainees were told to gather everything they owned and move out of the barracks. Once outside and in formation, Senior Lieutenant McKenzie held a roll-call in which he reformed the squads and sections assigning squad and team leaders, then the rest of the squad members. They were given the rest of the day off to rest and reorganize their gear before tactical training was to begin. The only person not assigned to a section was Titus, but he was told he would stay and attend the various classes, and could participate as desired in training.

Michael lost track of time as he along with his two Lieutenants became closer involved in teaching tactics and logistics to the Foresters. He returned from the field just before the mid-day meal to find he had a message from Altair. His son had been removed from the artificial womb and was doing well. Kaya was still improving but was now being kept in a medical induced coma, so they could start treatments on her to fix the genetic problems they had discovered. Since Kaya was not able to provide a name for the child and she had not decided on one before she went into the coma, it was asked of Michael what the child should be called.

He contacted Jiazi to find out what Kaya's father's name was. Michael sent a message back to Altair that his son would be named Makar Joseph Denoyelles. Makar was Kaya's father's name and Joseph was Michael's father. Duke Denoyelles had instructed that no release of information concerning the birth of Michael's child was to be issued as a measure of protecting the heir to the throne of Bellus, as the child was born with silver hair. Only Michael and Jiazi knew of the birth outside of the Duke.

A Haunting Pause

Three weeks into training, the trainees were standing in formation after a five-kilometer run in full field gear and weapons waiting to march over for their morning meal when a light swooshing sound was heard overhead. Suddenly, one, two, then three men landed on the open area in front of them, and right behind them more men came out of the sky.

Soon there were twenty-one combat ready men on the ground fanning out into a circular formation with weapons ready to take on any attacker. Michael walked out to the middle of this combat team and looked at the trainees.

"Foresters, these are Dark Horse Marines. What you have just witnessed is an insertion by parafoil to take, and secure a landing zone for the assault boats carrying the rest of the landing party. For the next three weeks these men are going to teach you everything you need to know about utilizing a parafoil from packing your own foil to a high altitude/low opening drop into any manner of landing zones during daylight or night. Gunny Greville is section leader and will take over training from Gunny Paxton. Gunny Greville, they are all yours."

One of the Marines rose up near the trainees and looked at them through his tinted face shield. His voice boomed out from the speakers in his helmet.

"Everyone close in on me, student mode."

The trainees had learned early on to form a semi-circle in front of an instructor with the front-rank kneeling as the back rank stood. Once the mode was formed, Greville retracted his face shield so everyone could see his face.

"Trainees, I am Gunny Greville, and for the next three weeks my men and I are going to give you five weeks of training. Do not hesitate to ask a question during instruction because the question you do not ask, might get yourself killed in a drop. Pay close attention to my men and they will give you the information you will need to safely drop from any altitude and live to brag about it to your friends or lovers. Take notice of the scar on my face. It is a constant reminder of my thinking I knew better than my instructors when I was a basic Marine. I have served with Captain Denoyelles when he was in the Dark Horse, and he will tell you I will not hesitate to ask a question, even if I know the answer in advance, just so my mind is secure with the knowledge contained within. You people do the same and you will find dropping from ten thousand meters is one big rush, and some of you might even laugh all the way to the ground from the enjoyment. Others might scream from fright, but if you can control that fear, apply it to the job at hand, then you will find you will overcome any fear of the drop. Now I understand the kitchen is ready to feed you so reassemble into formation. Move it people we are burning daylight!"

He released the trainees to go get chow, then moved back to pick up his own foil for repacking later. After the meal was finished Greville assigned two Marines per squad as instructors. The instructors moved their training squad away from the others which spread them out all over the open ground and began the initial training in nomenclature of the parafoil. Gunny Greville moved from group to group observing the training as it progressed.

During the mid-day meal, an assault boat landed with enough parafoils for each trainee. That afternoon, each individual deployed their foil on the ground, and laid them out with the instructors laying theirs out, and the first lessons in packing their own foil began.

Two days were spent just learning how to pack their foils with them being packed, unpacked, over and over until each instructor verified that each of their students had the operation down. Unlike Old Earth parachutes which could be unforgiving if a mistake was made in packing, the parafoils were very forgiving, but a mistake could happen.

From there the students learned how to land by jumping off tables until they were proficient, then they began jumping off the assault boats top deck. The trainees wore their foils everywhere they went and Gunny Greville might stop one and have them open their foil, then repack it under his critical eye. It was noticed that at night, the squads might open a foil and repack it, practicing what they have been learning. The instructors would stop in mid-lecture and ask a student a point about the foil which they were taught on the first day to see how well they had retained the knowledge.

The first jumps taken by the trainees were out of the back of a hovering assault boat at three hundred meters utilizing a static line attached to a taunt steel wire at the back of the boat. The parafoil deployed quick which gave the trainees plenty of time to prepare for the landing. Only two people hesitated on the first jump, but their squad mates pushed them out the boat before the instructors could assist them. Everyone made it to the ground unhurt and they repacked their foils and prepared for a second static line jump at six hundred meters later in the day. That night they jumped at a thousand meters without using the static line and using their sensor pack in their helmets to locate the center of the drop zone which was marked by a pulsing infrared marker.

Each day the jumps went higher until they had to use the emergency air supply in their helmets to breath as they dropped. No one drops from any altitude without the risk of injury, and on the sixth day two trainees were injured when one landed wrong, twisting a knee and another caught a sudden gust of wind and crashed into the assault boat on the ground loading up another group to take aloft to jump. Both were given two days rest and treatment before being allowed to make up their jumps and catch up with their squads.

Titus made enough jumps to be certified and backed away from the more difficult jumps since he knew he would never make a combat jump, but wanted to know what his people were dealing with.

At the end of the second week the trainees were given a day off while Michael and Greville looked at locations all over the planet to do training drops. Five locations were selected and the final week of parafoil training commenced before daylight the next day.

Training ended with a full unit jump over the Capital out of five assault boats with Michael and Titus leading the drop. The trainees made the drop as if a combat drop and secured the drop zone before a crowd of citizens and the Council. Once secure they gathered their foils and marched to where the Council was observing from the Cathedral steps. Jiazi acting as Chancellor presented each trainee with Badges representing the Bellus Security Force, then badges representing their qualification with the Parafoil.

Ten trainees were selected for additional training and promoted to the BSF rank of Sergeant. The rest of the trainees were given two weeks leave before returning to the training site for promotions and section formation. It was announced that in two months a new group would go through the training with fellow Foresters acting as instructors with the Marines supervising the training.

The ten trainees that returned to the training site were told they would be the new trainers based on how well they did through the training. They took a day's rest before the Marines began getting them ready to take over the mission of building a Security Force.

Michael was looking at a holo-map of the mountains to the south as he was planning war games for when the first group returned in a week. He found what he thought would be a good place to hold the games and expanded the view to get a better look at when Virna spoke from behind him.

"Captain Denoyelles, why are you looking at that part of the southern mountains?"

"Specialists Virna, I'm considering using this location for our next field exercise."

"Oh no Lord Denoyelles, we cannot go there! It is forbidden!"

Michael knew something was very wrong as none of the Foresters had ever called him anything except Captain. He was tempted to enter her mind, but held to the fact he was uncomfortable with his ability to do just that. Michael decided not to chastise her for using a title instead of his rank since he heard fear in her voice.

"Virna, explain yourself. Why is it forbidden?"

"It is haunted Sire. The Masters placed a ban on we Bellusarians from going there because of the demons that live in those mountains."

"Virna, has no one ever gone there to see if this was true?"

"We've heard tales of travelers losing their way into those mountains and never returning. Hunters will tell you they avoid those mountains even though they are plentiful with game because of demons that speak to them, taunt them to enter and die."

"That is interesting Virna. I will keep your words of warning in mind."

Just before daylight the next day, Michael boarded an assault boat with Gunny Greville and his section already on board, ready to combat drop into the Southern mountains.

A Ship Named Jilena

When Duke Denoyelles returned to Hanover to address the Federation Congress concerning the discovery of Bellus and the quarantine his grandson had placed on it, he also took a step which he felt was necessary for the preservation of the people of Bellus.

He ordered his fast freighter, Genevieve, to the Denoyelles shipyards for refit and modification. Being the head of the wealthiest family in the Federation, and owning the shipyards gave him the luxury to do what he felt was necessary and proper. The fact the Altairians only had one research vessel available to them bothered him.

The vessel was one of the largest in the Denoyelles fleet and was capable of landing at any space port in the Federation. As the ship was being stripped of its interior and refurbished for laboratories, the engines were being replaced with engines normally reserved for the Fleets Heavy Cruisers. These engines would give the vessel nearly three times its range before refueling, and increased its speed by an estimated forty-two percent.

The exterior was stripped of the Denoyelles Shipping colors and painted a high gloss white with a massive red cross at angles where they could be seen from almost any approach. Computers and communications were improved. By the time Makar Denoyelles was born, the Duke had spent enough money on this one ship to build three others.

The ship was rechristened the "Jilena" after his mother who had been treated by the Altairian's for a similar condition which Kaya was suffering from.

Its shakedown cruise was to Altair with a platoon of Lancers on board to insure its safety, and the safety of the two passengers it was to pick up, once the Altairians had outfitted the ship with the equipment and materials to make it a proper research vessel. Equipment and materials paid for by the Hanover Foundation. The run to Altair took six weeks instead of the normal eight and the

Captain of the Jilena reported he was only running at eighty percent boost.

Into the Mountains

As Michael stepped out of the assault boat at three thousand meters above the drop zone, he was unaware that Kaya and his son were aboard the Jilena and boosting out of orbit from Altair enroute to Bellus, with the Frigate Rostislav as escort. Kaya was stable, but in a medically induced coma as she was undergoing gene replacement therapy, and Makar was growing strong.

Michael never admitted to anyone he was scared of heights, but loved the sensation of free falling during a drop. He dropped to five hundred meters and released his parafoil, checked it, then release his drop bag as he adjusted his drop angle to glide into the small meadow high up on the mountain.

He was one hundred meters off the deck when his AI notified him at it had received a scan from an unknown source. The AI had fixed the direction that the scan had come from but could not pin point the origin of the scan. Michael turned in the direction of the scan and prepared for the landing.

Upon touching down, he took two steps to insure his drop bag was clear and dropped into the prone position as he moved his carbine into firing position in case he had to protect the men behind him. Moments later a Marine dropped to his left facing the same direct then another to his right. Michael's AI gave him a body count as each Marine touched down. He had his AI fix the direction of the scan and send it to all the AI's in the drop detail, then waited for several minutes as the AI counted three more scans on their position.

Michael gave the command for scouts out and three men moved from their coverage positions, following the direction the scan came from. From that point on, Gunny Greville coordinated the movement of his section with Michael gathering his drop bag, putting his field pack on and joining the movement in the middle of the section.

The scouts had barely gone one hundred meters when a voice could be heard echoing across the meadow warning them to flee before the mountain beast could devour them. The AI advised

Michael that the voice was mechanical in tone and texture. Only Michael could understand what was being said as it was in a version of the Bellusarian language.

Greville stopped the movement then sent three men to the right for one hundred meters and three men to the left and waited for another scan. It was several minutes before they were scanned again. This time they had the direction fixed from three different positions and that information was sent to both Michael's and Greville's AI's where the information was coordinated to pin point the source of the scan.

The scouts were fed the location of the scan and the movement proceeded at a pace which seemed slow to the common man, but was being taken in caution as the scouts looked for anything which might endanger them. The terrain was broken with no signs of travel by creature or man as they moved forward. The voice called out its warning again, then another sound was heard, a mechanical sound of movement.

At approximately ten meters away from the location, the scouts were greeted by a monster rising from the earth. It had the head of a grotesque creature with long fans and red eyes. It's four arms were moving in a jerking fashion and the two long tentacles erupting from its back were drooping, attempting to move without success. The fire discipline of the Marines was tested and found to be as it should, because it was obvious this was not a live monster, but a mechanical one due to the missing pieces of covering from its mechanical body shining in the morning light.

Regardless of the fact this was a machine and not a living creature, the scouts pulled back in order that if it was also an explosive device a modest distance might protect them, and they fanned out and went to ground.

As the rest of the Marines moved up and spread out watching in all directions for harm, Michael boldly walked to the monster as his AI was reading the composition of the beast. He carefully walked around the construct, staying just out of reach of the tentacles that were still trying to move and examined the monster.

Michael's AI informed him there was a panel on the back of the mechanism and outlined it on Michael's face shield. He stepped in and tried to pry it open with his fingers, and when that failed, he pulled his combat knife from his leg sheath and rammed the blade into the crack of the panel door and popped it open. Inside he found a simple switch and forced it to the opposite direction it was facing, and the sounds and movement of the mechanism ceased.

Looking inside the panel Michael could see writing in a language related to the Bellusarian language. He smiled to himself as he closed the panel, then made a call to the Heavy Destroyer Panborne.

"Panborne, this is Survey One, do you copy?"

"Survey One, this is Panborne we read you loud and clear."

"Panborne, Survey One requests you lock onto my position and tell me what your scanners are telling you."

"Survey One, Stand-by."

Michael knew that if he just called them with his rank they would go through several layers of channels before his request was fulfilled. But as Survey One for the Bellus Planet, he received instant support.

"Survey One, this is Panborne. We have you and a section of Marines clearly fixed. We also have some type of mechanical device next to you, and we are reading a Q-Wave power system emitting from it."

This brought a smile from Michael since Q-Waves were often mistaken for background radiation instead of power sources.

"Panborne, I need three things. First scan this mountain range from the foothills to the peaks for Q-Wave radiation focusing on the strongest readings at each location found. Second, I need a deep scan looking for tunnels or bunkers. Specifically tunnels entrances. Do you understand my request?"

"Affirmative Survey One, we copy deep scan for tunnels and entrances and to pin-point Q-Wave sources. What is the third item you need?"

"Panborne, I need a platoon of Marines at my location with sapper capability as soon as you can get them loaded."

There was a long silence before Panborne responded.

"Survey One, be advised all requests for Marines on the ground has to come through either Duke Denoyelles with concurrence of the Bellus Council."

"Panborne, do you have contact with Bellus?"

"Affirmative Survey One."

"Notify them that Prince Michael Denoyelles has ordered you to drop a platoon of Marines at my location, and while you are doing that load those Marines up and get them moving this way."

Again, there was a long silence.

"Survey One this is Panborne Actual. Do I understand that I am dropping a platoon of my Marines on the orders of the Throne of Bellus?"

"Panborne Actual that is correct. Captain Sabella, have you been briefed on my relationship to the Throne?"

"Affirmative Survey One. I was just insuring I was not starting a war on Bellus."

"Negative Panborne, any war here on Bellus will be between myself and the Council in private chambers, and it will be bloodless. Do you accept your instructions Panborne?"

"Survey One, be advise we have a platoon forming on the hanger deck at this time, and prepping for sapper operations. They will be instructed to land at your drop zone as soon as we can get them out of the hanger."

"Thank you Panborne. Survey One out."

Michael could not get upset with Panborne Actual, the Captain of the Panborne in covering his ass considering the quarantine on the planet. There was no doubt that Captain Sabella was having their conversation extracted to a memory cube and a hard copy printed to go into his Captain's Log in case someone raises a stink about deploring Marines without consulting the Duke or the Council.

An hour later Michael was briefing the platoon beside their assault boat. A Marine Platoon is made up of two sections plus the Platoon Leader, Platoon Gunny and a communications specialist. Michael had the sections broken down into their five-man teams and each team was given a location of the Q-Waves found by the Panborne.

Michael informed them what they had found and what the teams would likely find. They were to use extreme caution in approaching any mechanical monster they might find in case others were more active than the one they had found. He did not want them destroyed, only disabled unless the safety of the team was involved. Report all discoveries back to the Platoon Leader, Senior Lieutenant Thrasher.

Gunny Greville and his section were able to remove the mechanism from its base and moved it down the mountain to the meadow for transport. Michael contacted McKenzie and had him bring his survey shuttle to pick up the monster, so they could take it back to the Capital.

Michael's AI was notifying him of messages from the training camp and Capital wanting to know what he was doing in the Southern mountains, but he ignored them until he was ready to face the Council with his discovery.

One discovery Greville made while dismounting the mechanical monster was that the tentacles were light and easy to move. He passed that information to all the teams moving about the mountain, so they would be aware that while they looked dangerous, other than a man being knocked down by them, they appeared to be only for show. Also, the large hands on the arms had a limited range of movement meaning they most likely could not grip and tear a person, but even though the claws were blunted, dull, they could still cause harm.

Michael flew to the Capital with McKenzie and a team of Marines to assist in moving the mechanism once at the Capital to show to the Council. He was ready to be chastised for his use of his title after he had sworn to never use it, but Michael also knew there were times a man had to go back on his word to accomplish what others feared.

Bellus Control instructed Michael to land on the pad in front of the Cathedral where he saw the Council standing on the steps awaiting him. Titus was dressed in the new uniform of the BSF with a team of BSF troops standing behind the Council.

Michael exited the shuttle and walked directly to Jiazi who was standing forefront of the Council. He came to the position and saluted her.

"Lady Jiazi, I have something for the Council which was found in the southern mountains."

"Yes, Captain Denoyelles or should we call you Prince Michael, now since you used the title to order a full, combat ready platoon of Marines to the surface in violation of the agreement between the Council, and the Duke, your Grand-Father. You also violated Bellusarian Law in going into the southern mountains, which I have been inform that Specialist Virna advised you that such travel was forbidden."

"Lady Jiazi, as Commander Titus can tell you from the training he has completed, decisions made in real time on a battle field must be made to accommodate the situation the commander in the field has to face. I extend my apologizes to the Council for making such decisions, but I am not trained in the art of diplomacy, but in the art of war. I can only hope that which I have brought to the Capital in my shuttle will explain my actions."

"Captain Denoyelles, Commander Titus did inform the Council concerning the need to bypass proper channels when faced

144

by uncertainty. We will hold his comments in mind as we view that which you felt required you to violate the agreement made by the Duke. Show us what you have discovered."

Michael touched the side of his helmet and ordered the mechanism removed from the shuttle. The Marines brought the mechanism out and faced it towards the Council. Michael pointed to it as he spoke.

"Council, this is the monster which inhabits the southern mountains. Yes, Specialist Virna advised me that the southern mountains were forbidden, but never told me why other than they were haunted. I have seen too many things in my short life to believe in ghosts. To avoid the mountains because of monsters was another myth given to you by the Masters, and this mechanism was built by the Masters to enforce that myth. The last report I received from the Marines on the mountain is that they have disabled thirteen other mechanisms like this one."

"Captain Denoyelles, what makes you believe the Masters constructed this thing before us?" Lady Jiazi asked.

"Because of the writing inside the access panel on its back. It is in the form of the Bellusarian language which I have been told was also the language of the Masters. Lady Jiazi, there is something in those mountains the Masters did not want your people to discover. But I think it is time for your people, our people to move out of the darkness of the Master."

Jiazi walked down to take a closer look at this monster with the Council following. Michael opened the back of the mechanism, so everyone could see, and read the writing inside the panel. The Council spoke in hushed whispers as they talked amongst themselves concerning this discovery. Titus moved to Michael to speak with him.

"Captain Denoyelles, I think I know the answer, but why did you take Marines with you to the mountains instead of BSF members?

"Commander Titus, I took Marines for various reasons. But like myself, they are not infected with the taboos of going into those mountains. The Marines are trained not to react to the unknown, but to act on it. When this creature rose from the ground, the Marines did not fire upon it until they were certain of the danger. Since there was no danger, they held their fire giving me the chance to examine it as it was under power, then to basically turn it off. The BSF still have a lot to learn, and they are learning their lessons well, but they would have shot this thing to pieces before I could have regained control of them."

"Yes, Captain Denoyelles, I see your logic in this matter. Even with the technology we have at our fingertips, we are still in many ways a backward people. I believe your people would say we have been spoon fed mythology for so many generations, that it has become part of our reality. We do have so much to learn."

The Council regathered at the foot of the Cathedral steps and discussed the situation and Michael's conduct both as the planets Survey Officer and as the Prince. Jiazi once more faced Michael with the Council's decision.

"Captain Denoyelles, it has been debated, and determined that your use of your Princely title was well within your oath not to take the Throne in the absence of the Princess, nor was it an attempt to usurp the Council, but was a decision made in consideration of the safety and security of the people of Bellus. The Council thanks you for bringing this new information directly to us. What is your next move concerning the southern mountains?"

"Lady Jiazi, I would like to take Commander Titus and a squad back to the mountains as support to the Marines already roaming the mountains. This will also show the Bellusarian people there is nothing to fear from the mountains, and to also learn from the Marines in action there."

"Commander Titus?" Jiazi asked.

"Lady Jiazi, I can have a squad ready in twenty minutes. I would like to see these mountains that we have been told to fear."

"So be it Commander Titus. Captain Denoyelles, a moment of your time in private please."

Jiazi moved off the steps away from the Council with Michael following.

"Michael, I know you have been ignoring communications since you went to the mountain, and I am not in position to be critical of that since it appears you had other things on your mind."

"Yes Jiazi, I will be honest in that if I had answered your messages, I may have ignored your instructions and continued which would have greatly offended you, so I just ignored the messages."

"Well Michael one message you ignored was the message that our Kaya is returning home along with Makar. They boosted from Altair this morning in a new ship the Duke has provided for the Altairians. He calls it a hospital ship, and we will begin construction a special landing pad for it due to its size and weight. We should be ready when they arrive. The Duke said the name of the ship is the Jilena, and you would know the meaning of the name."

Michael lightly laughed.

"Mother Jiazi, Jilena is the name of the Duke's mother who also had a genetic problem in childbirth. The Altairians cured Jilena otherwise my Grand-Father may have never been born."

"Then the ship is well named."

Michael lifted off in less time than Titus gave him as a squad of BSF troops loaded onto the shuttle ready for action. Titus briefed them enroute and calmed their fears when he explained that the Marines were already on the ground and what they were finding was not what they had been raised to believe.

Instead of landing in the original meadow, Michael landed in a small area high up on the mountain where he was met by three teams of Marines already on site. According to the Panborne, there was a tunnel entrance at that location which appeared to be buried by a rock slide. McKenzie took the shuttle and picked up the rest of Greville's section and returned to just drop them off, then back to the original drop zone to await further orders.

Greville, his two squad leaders and four other Senior Sergeants moved to the debris covering the tunnel entrance and discussed the best way to remove it. Once they agreed on a course of action, they fell back to Michael's position and explained what they felt they needed to do. The shuttle was brought in and began to lift Marines back to the drop zone while Greville and two Senior Sergeants took four of the BSF troops up to the rock slide to prepare charges to blow as much of the debris away as possible.

The Marines supervised the BSF people as they prepped the charges, then emplaced them with remote detonators. Michael and Titus were at the slide observing. Michael could feel the nervousness coming from Titus as he stood so close to large amounts of explosives being handled by inexperienced troops.

Once the charges were set, everyone left loaded onto the shuttle and flew off to the estimated safe distance, hovered in place as the rear ramp of the shuttle was lowered for everyone to watch the explosion. Michael announced over the radio he was blowing the charges, then counted three before flipping the switch on the remote detonator.

The view of the rock slide became obscured by the dust and debris flying out away from the rock slide. Large boulders could be seen rolling down the mountainside as smaller rocks became ballistic missiles flying in all directions. As they dust began to settle, McKenzie moved back to the area to drop his cargo of men and two women off, so he could collect the rest of the Marines to return them to the tunnel entrance.

One of the first things Michael noticed was the dull shine of metal from where the entrance of the tunnel was supposed to be located. Yes, Michael thought, it did have a door, but would it open after all the time closed without breaching tools?

As Michael moved to the tunnel entrance and began climbing over debris, he heard Greville talking to the BSF troops about the effect of the explosions and how it forced the debris away from the entrance without any visible damage to the entrance itself or causing further rock slides.

Michael moved to a point where he could see the entrance better and knew that they would soon be inside once the others arrived and began clearing the last of the debris away from the door. But he also knew soon was objective because there was still a lot of material to be moved.

Lieutenant Thrasher put the Marines to work as they arrived removing the debris. Michael lost track of Titus for a bit until he located him working beside his BSF troops in moving rocks from the entrance. The Panborne had taken up a stationary orbit above the tunnel entrance and were constantly scanning to insure the safety of the Marines working the site.

The work was slow, and Thrasher was moving men around to ease their labors as they were working to gain the entrance to the tunnel. He shut them down after two hours to take a long break and eat a ration. The Marines warned the BSF troops to eat light and save their rations for the evening meal since this kind of labor on a full stomach would not only slow them down, but could make them sick.

It was almost nightfall when Thrasher felt the entrance was cleared and safe enough to attempt to open the tunnel. The Panborne had been monitoring for any activity inside the tunnel and had reported zero activity, and no increase in Q-Wave activity within the tunnel complex that could be read with the scanners.

Michael ordered everyone down to the small level area where the shuttle could land so it could bring in hot chow for the Marines and BSF. He told Titus they would make camp at that location, then try to open the tunnel in the morning.

A duty watch was set with two Marines and a BSF trooper standing watch together on two-hour cycles. Michael finally had a chance to consider how he felt about Kaya coming back to him and bringing their son with her. What he did not know was that she was still in a medically induced coma while undergoing treatment.

149

A Peek into the Past

Michael was at the entrance to the tunnel before the shuttle arrived with the morning meal. He searched every centimeter of the exposed metal door looking for a control panel of any type. His AI enhanced his vision as best it could without risking damage to Michael's eyes. Nothing could be found making Michael come to the conclusion that the door was either meant to never be opened, or it was opened from the inside.

During the meal, Michael told Lieutenant Thrasher they would have to use a breaching charge at the center of the door. Thrasher told Michael they would get right on it once everyone had finished chow. The breaching charges Michael referred to were designed to cut through armored bulkheads on ships without damaging what was on the other side. There were different versions of this charge and Thrasher decided to go with the Type IV charge which would cut through thirty centimeters of armor plate.

The entire BSF group including Titus, were taken to the entrance and a short class was held concerning the utilization of a breaching charge. The charge was set two hand widths above the ground, a meter across and two meters from its lowest point. A remote detonator was set to it, then everyone moved back fifty meters from the entrance and went to ground.

A breaching charge does not explode through metal as it burns through it. Because of this there is very little noise accompanying the detonation of the charge. Michael hit the remote then counted ten before rising from the ground, and moving towards the smoldering entrance. In the entrance was a hole outlined in the metal plate blocking the entrance, but the piece of plate which was cut out had not fallen away.

Michael moved to the cut-out and kicked it hard with the heel of his boot. It moved, and he kicked it a second time and it fell into the tunnel entrance. Michael never looked to see if he was being followed as he stepped into the tunnel and moved forward to allow others to follow him.

He stopped about five paces into the tunnel as his AI gave him a gold tint to the darkness via the enhanced vision it provided. The walls and tunnel floor were smooth, finished and sealed insuring they were stable from rock falls. As he studied the tunnel, Marines and BSF troops moved past him and slowly began to move down the tunnel ahead of him.

Titus walked up beside Michael.

"Lord Prince, what are your orders?"

"Titus, you ever call me that again outside of the Council chambers, and I will test your ability with a sword. Do you understand my instructions?"

"Michael, my apologies, but you have taken our people beyond superstition into the real world. I only meant it as a manner of respect. My steel is yours to command, Captain Denoyelles."

"Commander Titus, form up your command and follow the Marines in support. Pass the word that they are to keep their weapons on safe unless the Marines become engaged in a fight. This is a good learning exercise for them."

"As you command, Captain."

Titus moved away issuing instructions to his people over their radio frequency as more Marines moved past Michael. Lieutenant Thrasher had already moved past and was controlling the movement into the mountain. When they came to a connecting tunnel, Thrasher posted two Marines to watch it as it was being bypassed. Titus then posted two of his people to support the Marines with instructions to follow the orders of the Marines.

Six additional connecting tunnels were located as they moved further into the mountain, beyond the abilities of the Panborne scanners to watch their progress. The point elements had gone just over a kilometer into the mountain when they halted, as they found themselves looking into a large, open cavern that they could not see the other side.

Michael walked past the point men and looked into the cavern as far as he could, then walked back to the entrance and spoke to Titus and Thrasher.

"We need to get lights down here and see what we have. And the connecting tunnels need to be lighted and inspected. Lieutenant Thrasher, contact the Panborne to coordinate lighting and some blowers. The air is foul and will only get worse as we move about stirring the dust on the walls and floor. And Thrasher, if they complain, advise then that Commander Titus of the BSF is on site and has requested those items."

Titus laughed and nodded his agreement. Thrasher took off at a trot to go back to the surface, so he would have a clear line of communications to the Panborne.

An hour later the first shuttle landed with the blowers and Navy engineers to operate and maintain them as the Marines were busy inside the mountain. Additional holes were burned into the steel door to allow blowers to pump fresh air into the tunnel with larger holes burned in near the top of the door as exhaust ports. Another hole was burned for when the light sets arrived, so their power lines could be passed through without interfering with the opening which was also enlarged making it half again taller and twice as wide. It was also cut to ground level so there would be ease of access.

As the connecting tunnels were being lighted, the detail on each tunnel moved ahead of the Navy engineers. They found doors leading off the tunnels, but no matter what they tried, the access panels for these doors would not power up to open the doors. The Marines attached warning devices to the doors in case they opened behind them.

When Titus asked Michael why he was lighting the tunnels before the cavern, Michael just smiled at him. Titus recognized that smile as figure it out for himself. After a moment's thought Titus said by lighting the tunnels he was securing his rear before he advanced any further. Michael clapped him on the shoulder and gave Titus an approving nod.

The Navy engineers were working as fast as they could, but the Chief Engineer advise Michael it may not be until mid-day the next day before they could begin to light the cavern due to the depths of some of the tunnels and the number of lights they had brought down. He had already requested additional lights, and those would be coming from other ships as soon as they could break them out of the holds and transport them to the surface.

The small landing area was becoming so crowded with shipping cases that when a shuttle or assault boat off loaded a new load of lights, the empty containers already on the ground were loaded up to be taken back to any ship they ended up on. As this was happening, the Panborne notified Fleet Headquarters of the expenditure of the light sets so they could be replaced if the ones on the ground were to be left in place.

Captain Sabella of the Panborne had an assault boat loaded with a field kitchen and dispatched with volunteer cooks to take care of the men on the ground. When Titus found out he sent a message to the Panborne to thank them for the consideration.

A door was opened in one of the tunnels and the Marines waited until Michael could arrive before entering. It appeared to be a large storage room with crates lining both walls. Titus could not make out the markings on the boxes and it was decided to wait until later to remove them and open them in a safer environment.

The second door that was found to open was an even larger room with what appeared to be machinery to product some unknown objects. That door was sealed for later examination.

That evening, the Marines emplaced sensors to detect any movement within the tunnels so a small detail could be posted at the tunnel entrance to keep watch overnight allowing the others to rest.

Michael had trouble sleeping and got up to go check on the detail, even though he knew the Marines would be alert and would keep the BSF people awake. When he entered the tunnel, he found Titus with the detail talking to his people.

"Commander Titus, are you also having trouble finding sleep this night?"

"Yes, Captain Denoyelles, I am. I must admit in front of our men that I feel guilty that they are working long hours, while I just stand around observing their efforts."

"Commander, I understand your feelings. As a Cadet Lieutenant, my Sergeants worked me hard, but as I gained promotions, I found I had less to do unless we were engaged with an enemy. Commander, what you have to remember is that what you are observing is Sergeant's business, and we officers should never interfere with it unless we change the plan they have been given, and are working under."

"I agree Captain Denoyelles, as I have been observing your Marines as they go about their assignments. The major things are obvious, but they seem to know small things which passed me by at first."

"Yes, Commander, those little things come from experience. Something most officers never achieve because they are never allowed to spend that amount of time at the Sergeant's level of business. In time, your Sergeants will learn and become the strength of the BSF."

Michael returned to his sleeping pad and fell asleep without difficulty.

Change of Command

The old Navy Chief who oversaw the installation of the lights, had ordered man-moveable scaffolding as soon as he saw the heights of the tunnels. The ceiling in the main tunnel was just barely over six meters above the floor and the side tunnels about four meters high. The Marines became the manpower to move the scaffolding and hustle more cable and fixtures as the Navy engineers attached the lights to the ceiling.

The last side tunnel was being lit as the main tunnel was finished. The Chief walked into the cavern with a power-cell powered hand-held spot light and aimed it at the ceiling. The ceiling was curved with the spot above tunnel entrance estimated to be thirty meters high. But the one thing the Chief noticed was the reflection of the light around the cavern. He ordered one of the high intensity spot lights that was brought to the surface to light the exterior of the mountain at the tunnel entrance to be moved into the cavern.

Once the light was in position and hooked into the main power feed, the Chief turned it on and moved the beam until it was shining directly on the peak of the cavern ceiling. This caused the entire cavern to light up as if it was daylight inside.

Michael, Titus, Thrasher, and the Gunny's all stood looking at the contents of the cavern. There were ground vehicles and an odd assortment of equipment parked in the cavern. It also appeared on the far side were small flying craft of unknown origin. They heard the Chief mutter at they had to send for more light kits since they could see four more tunnels around the rim of the cavern.

When Michael took a step forward to begin his exploration of the cavern, Titus grasped his arm, holding him back.

"Sorry Captain Denoyelles, your mission here is over. I'm taking command of this operation as per instructions of the Council of Bellus."

"Commander Titus, you have no experience in room clearing such as this is."

155

"Captain Denoyelles, unless you wish to proclaim royal privilege, we both must accept the Councils ruling. Besides, how else will I, or my Rangers get the experience?"

"Your Rangers?"

"Yes, Rangers. Last night during the evening meal I was talking to Lieutenant Thrasher and he mentioned that on his world, Foresters were known as Rangers. He also told me that at one time on Earth, there was a military unit on the North American Continent that were known as Rangers. I believe it is a good title for the Foresters you have trained and will train. Do you not agree?"

"Yes Commander, I agree. I have read about the old Earth Rangers. So, what now Commander?"

"I have ordered my Rangers to form at the Cathedral where Jiazi will brief them concerning the myths of this mountain, then they will board transport carriers and report here. We will take over what you and your Marines have been doing as the primary force, but if you would, I think Marine advisors with my teams could provide advice and training for my future leaders."

"Since I will not claim royal privilege, as soon as your Rangers are on the ground, I will surrender command and remove my Marines. And to keep this polite, I will not venture any further into the cavern without an invitation."

"Thank you Captain Denoyelles, and I would be forever grateful if you would be on hand to advise me from time to time and remind me I have much to learn."

"One question."

"Certainly Captain."

"Why did you try to separate myself and Kaya with those nightmares?"

Titus jerked his head towards Michael who was just looking out into the cavern.

"Because Kaya is the most beautiful woman I have ever seen. I desired her as any man could. Michael, I tried to talk her out of following through with her father's project, but as you well know she can be stubborn, especially where her people are concerned. I wanted her Michael, not the crown, but as Gunny Greville likes to say, the throne was icing on the cake. Once this is over if you wish to challenge me, I'll understand."

"Do you love her Titus?"

"No Michael, but my desire was strong. Strong enough to act irresponsibly by trying to frighten you off as I did. Baron Denoyelles, you have my most sincere apology."

"Lord Titus, I accept your apology. Now, let's post a couple of Rangers here and wait until the rest of your people arrive before we go take a look at what the Masters have left us."

Discoveries

Michael had stood and watched as the BSF Rangers formed up and were briefed by Titus. When he pronounced their new name and the history of it that he was aware of, it seemed to boost their pride. A Marine was assigned per five-man team with the understanding they were to observe and advise, but to stay out of their way, and let them make all the mistakes possible, as long as no one was hurt in making those mistakes.

He sent Gunny Greville and his section to the training site to assist McKenzie as another one hundred Foresters were due to report for training. It had been his plan to train Foresters/Rangers to take over the training, but Titus needed every individual to secure the mountain and search for those mechanical monsters the Marines had yet to disable.

The equipment contained within the cavern was in nearly perfect condition except their power sources had long since either died, or as one engineer noted, had been removed. Once it was determined there was no danger from the equipment stored in the cavern, the new tunnels were explored and lighted.

Six weeks after Michael kicked the door open to the tunnel, the Duke came to the cavern for a visit. With him came the Council to see what had been discovered and what was still to be done. The field kitchen had been set up in the cavern and there was a meeting utilizing the tables for dining.

This meeting was as much a business meeting as it was to learn what had been discovered. The Duke found himself in a very uncomfortable position of having to inquire how the Bellusarians were going to pay for the equipment they were using and the rations for the men. The Federation Council and Congress waved the wages for the men, but the other items still had to be replaced.

It was quickly discovered that the Bellusarian people had no real grasp of money. They had inherited a communal lifestyle from the Masters in which everyone worked to support their neighbor. Jiazi pointed out that Kaya was a prime example of their system in that even though she was considered a Princess, royalty, and heir to the throne, she worked at being a Forester which helped control the animal life on the planet, she would also take and animal or two, if word came to her that there was a need for meat protein within the community.

She went on to give more examples of how their system worked by describing what each Council member did when not sitting to discuss the needs of the community.

But since the planet was still under quarantine, trade had yet to be established which meant no influx of currency from off planet to fund projects such as was taking place on the mountain. The Duke finally asked if the planet had any precious metals or gem stones which was met with confusion by the Council. It took the Duke removing a gold coin from his purse and laying it on the table before the Council understood what he meant.

To the Bellusarians, gold was just another metal to be formed and used as needed. The Duke would discover later in the day that Bellus was rich in gold and silver. The only problem the Bellusarians had was finding the common weight measurement so they could smelt the gold into the proper weight bricks, so they could pay the growing debt with the Federation.

Later, the Duke went with Michael to check on things at the training camp. The discussion started in flight, but got serious after they landed while secluded in the shuttle.

"Alright Michael, there is something bothering you, yet you are holding it inside. Speak your mind."

"Grandfather, the Bellusarians have a near perfect society here. Everyone is cared for and have no wants more than they need. Once the planet is open to trade, to travelers, what becomes of them? How will they adapt to the influence of Federation Crowns coming to them to purchase what goods they decide to make and sell?"

"Michael, that is one of my main concerns also. My father had that same concern when he established the Hanover Foundation in that he might turn those struggling into individuals who would stop trying and allow the government to provide for them. He picked the right man to head the Foundation when he picked Lord Strahovski as Chancellor to the Throne. But to be honest we have greater worries with the Bellusarians."

"Such as?" Michael asked.

"First, there is their ability to read minds. Control minds with their psychic powers. I am aware of their laws concerning the use of those powers to influence others, but once greed takes hold here from the flow of money into the planets economy, will they be able to control that talent?"

"Yes, Grandfather, but I believe this generation will keep the next couple of generations in line, but after that I have no idea how things will turn out. What's next on your list?"

"Their cloaking devices. Michael, I know you are unaware of this, but the word is already out. About a month ago, some scavengers were captured raiding the Fleets dump on Crandall's moon. They claim they came here and met you. According to their statements, you vanished before their eyes, then reappeared in another spot as you warned them off the planet. Federation Intelligence has taken their statements and compared them to the statements of the slavers that brought Bellus to our attention. One thing that the Federation has noted is there is no mention of your meeting the scavengers in your daily reports."

"Grandfather I did not report that meeting because we both know, if it was not written down, not reported, it never happened. But here is a secret I have not shared with you. Their cloak can be defeated by their own technology. Kaya gave me a small device that adhered to my helmet that worked with my AI, and I could see her cloaked as I could see her vehicle. It worked with my night vision element to basically enlighten her regardless what time of the day it was. The Foresters carry what looks like glasses, so they can see each other when working as teams. But I'm concerned that someone will get their cloak and improve on it to the point that detection is near impossible."

"Michael, I agree that can be a real problem, especially if one of the independent mercenary groups lays their hands on it. As Marines, we are both aware of how dangerous that can be especially in some bush war. A light company could wipe out a heavy battalion in a very short time. Any suggestions?"

"Currently the only people who have the cloak are Foresters, and of course the one that cloaked the Capital, and the smaller communities. Kaya said the reason they used the cloak was, so they would not disturb the animals as they studied them. Makes great sense all things considered, but the technology exists regardless who uses it. May I make a suggestion that could solve several problems as once?"

"Certainly Michael, what is it?"

"I think that if the Federation offers the Bellusarians enough money, they just might destroy every one of their cloaking devices and the technology to reproduce it. This puts a healthy reserve into the planets coffers while removing one of the greatest threats to the university in a millennium. Granted the Fleet could make good use of such a device in their fight against slavers, but if one fell into the hands of those same slavers, then they could raid at will."

"Michael, I believe this is something a Prince should handle for his people."

"Grandfather, you know how I feel about using that title."

"Michael, do you think I like being referred to as the Duke? My father hated both being the Count and the Duke, but it was a tool he used to bring about change. Someday, if the saints are willing, you'll carry the burden of being the Duke."

"I'll need to talk to Kaya before I can even think about using my title here. Being the Baron Denoyelles was all well and good since it is a ceremonial title, but being the Prince of Bellus is a whole different matter."

The Duke laughed before commenting on what Michael had said.

"Michael, I hate to destroy the image of yourself, but as Baron Denoyelles, you are wealthier than some planets in the Federation. Our ancestors were greedy, but created a financial empire that only builds upon itself decade after decade. My father found good people to run the family's businesses and insured everyone from the lowest person working for him was treated with the same respect as the managing director. This bred a system where innovation was rewarded regardless of who it was that brought the idea to light. One of the companies that you own was started using the idea of a file clerk. Even after she became wealthy from her share of the revenue, she continued to work in files until she retired."

"Why is it I did not know about my wealth?"

"Because it is not yours until you leave the Marines. My father did this to me and I did this to your father while he was in the Fleet, commanding destroyers. We manage your interests, so you do not have to concern yourself with them while serving. And before you ask, no, you cannot touch your wealth until you leave service. Michael, this is done so you understand the value of what you work for. And to be honest this was not my father's idea but my mothers. You've read my father's book, so you might understand what I am saying to you."

"Why are you telling me this now?"

"Michael, it's because you are coming to a crossroads. Your enlistment is almost up, and you are now married to the throne of an independent planet. A planet which has no guidance to the future and zero experience dealing with those who will eventually come and try to take advantage of their innocence. Grandson, you have the wealth of generations behind you if you wish to use it to benefit your new family, the people of Bellus."

"Grandfather, I have no idea how to run a business much less an empire. I'm better at dealing with Marines than I am bureaucrats."

"Michael, the managers of your businesses know that they only have their jobs as long as the business is making money and

162

that the employees are being taken care of. They are loyal to the family and the company because they understand an audit can happen at any time, and the people we use to do the audits cannot be bought. All you have to do is let them do their job and do nothing that might mess up their system."

This gave Michael much to think about knowing Kaya and Makar were on their way home. As wealthy as the Denoyelles family was, his parents made him earn every Crown he put into his pocket. Even with servants in the house, he remembered having to put away his toys when finished with them, because his mother told him they were not paying the maids to pick up after him when he was capable of doing that himself.

Even then they were preparing him for this day or the day to come.

After checking on the training, Michael took his grandfather back to the Capital before returning to the mountain. The Marines, using the two open doors the found discovered an easy way of opening the doors without using a lot of explosives. A simple breaching charge strategically placed opened the doors. The Marines also used the two open rooms to teach the Rangers how to enter and clear a room. From that point, the process of opening the rooms from the main tunnel went quick.

The Rangers blew one door and entered what appeared to be a barracks stretching down to the next tunnel with an exit there which they opened from the inside without explosives. The single beds in the barracks looked as if they had been set up the day before without linen. The mattresses for the beds were made from an unknown material and formed to the body.

Off to either side of the barracks were sanitary facilities which gave everyone a nice surprise in that when a valve was opened, water came from the spout. There were two handles which was common in the universe for hot and cold water, but only cold water came from the spouts. And the longer the water ran, the colder it became which gave birth to the theory that the water was coming from higher up on the mountain, most likely from the snow or snow melt.

The Rangers began to notice the Marines were getting nervous as room after room was opened, until one asked if they were doing something wrong. The Marine's only comment was that the rooms were too clean, too neat to have been left abandoned for so long. He was waiting for someone to pop out from a hidden door.

No matter what the room contained it was neat and clean. Labs were as if they had just been set up, but unused. What appeared to be machine shops showed no signs of ever being used. No matter where they looked, the equipment seemed to be brand new and unused. But there was no power to the facilities and anything needing an internal power supply either had it removed or it was drained of power. And they could not locate any removed power supplies.

Bellusarian scientists entered the cavern to examine the equipment in the labs but could not determine the purpose of any lab. It was frustrating for the Rangers to work as hard as they had without any solid results to show for their labors.

When a large cafeteria was located complete with kitchen, the Navy's field kitchen was moved into that area until the engineers could figure out how to power up the cooking appliances and figured out a way to heat water for the faucets. The Rangers took over the kitchen at this point and gave a small party for the Navy as thanks. One Navy cook stayed behind to assist as the rations being prepared were standard Fleet rations which were unlike what the Bellusarians normally ate.

As the last lights were being hung, Rangers were being taught how to operate and maintain the power supplies for the lights and other items within the cavern. Section by section the Marines pulled out of the cavern and returned to their ships in orbit with the thanks of the Bellusarians.

Titus asked Michael if they could do anything else for the men who had trained and supported them during the time in the cavern. Michael explained that a letter of commendation for each

164

man's file would be helpful later when that man came up for promotion. Titus had Michael help him write letters for each man, Navy and Marine and signed them with his BSF rank and signature. This was almost laughable for Michael since Titus had to copy a single form letter written by Michael since Titus did not know how to write in Federation Standard.

The commendation packet was sent to the ships by the next supply shuttle to be distributed to each ship.

Two days later, the Altairian Hospital Ship Jilena entered orbit in preparation to landing at the Capital.

Reunion

Michael stood in the shade of his shuttle as the Jilena cooled from its landing orbit. He reached out to Kaya in his mind, but could not find her which worried him as he stood silently praying that it was him, and not something to be dreaded.

He did not hesitate as the ramp began to lower to the Jilena and he was met at the top of the ramp by Senior Lieutenant Alecia Bascalo, the head of Kaya's security detail.

"Captain Denoyelles. Sir, you are to go directly to Doctor Guillemot before meeting the Princess."

"Lieutenant Bascalo, did the doctor give you a reason for my meeting him first?"

"No Sir, but the Princess is awake and waiting for you once you meet with the Doctor. She is aware of the Doctor's orders Sir."

"And my son?"

"Sir, he is in the nursery with two of my detail and will be brought to you once you meet with the Princess."

Michael took a deep sigh before responding. He knew that resisting the orders of the doctor would only cause problems and then there was the fact that Lieutenant Bascalo worked for his Grandfather would create problems from that direction.

"Alright Lieutenant, lead the way please."

Bascalo led Michael through the ship and up four decks before she rapped on a door, opened it, then stepped aside for Michael to enter. Michael's first view of Doctor Guillemot was surprising. The doctor was an elderly female whose hair had turned white. She spoke before he did.

"Ah, Captain Denoyelles, please come in and sit down. We have a few things to discuss before you can meet your wife, the Princess Kaya."

"Just give me the bad news doctor, then allow me to see my wife."

Guillemot lightly laughed.

"Captain, please sit, there is no bad news. But you have not seen your wife in nearly a year, and I just wish that you know her condition at the moment."

As Michael sat down, Doctor Guillemot began.

"Captain, I have spent my life in DNA research. Your wife's situation took longer than anyone considered due to the nature of her DNA modification by those that are now called the Masters. In comparing your DNA to hers along with that of the Centaurians, it looks similar, but the reality is that your DNA was modified through reproduction whereas Kaya's was modified by the infusion of the Masters DNA in the laboratory. This tells those of that research DNA that the Masters were not adapt in such things."

"I'm not sure I'm following you doctor."

"We've extracted the Masters DNA from its link to human DNA and then broke it down as far as possible. Now I'm not using a lot of our technical or medical terms, so you'll understand, but what happened was the Masters infected the Bellusarians with the very defect that was killing their own race. One theory is they did this on purpose to study the results in hope to correct their own problems. But it did not seem to work as quick as they hoped since from what I have been told is that the Masters disappeared over a millennium ago while the decline if Bellusarian birth rate is relative new, say the past two hundred solar years."

"Where is this leading doctor?"

"When a female becomes pregnant, her body adjusts to having what is basically a parasite inside of it, and insures both bodies have what they need to survive. We have seen this before in other races due to a recessive gene such as your Grandmother Jilena had. But in the case of the Bellusarians, this is not a recessive gene which may stay dormant through several generations, but is an active one in both male and female."

She paused to let that sink in before continuing.

"In the case of the Bellusarians, it seems that the fetus truly becomes a parasite which the host is willing to support, but cannot support itself thus causing the host to die, often before the fetus matures and is born. This is why we removed your son from his mother. He was literally killing his mother as she was giving him everything he needed to grow."

"Why hasn't this effected the Centaurians if they also carry the Masters DNA?"

"As I said the Centaurians were transformed through intercourse, direct infusion of the Masters DNA via sperm, where the Bellusarians were injected with specific DNA. The human DNA only accepted those aspects of the Masters DNA that was capable with the human genome. The recessive DNA was rejected and ejected from the human host. Now this sounds simple, yet it is not, I'm just trying to keep this simple for you."

"Thank you doctor, but what about Kaya?"

"Kaya is recovering nicely, but has a long road to still yet travel before she is well enough to even consider having another child. And when that happens, she will carry to term as a normal human female. But before you see her understand, she is not the person that left you for Altair. She lost over fifty percent of her weight before we could stop and reverse the process which was killing her, so accept her as she is because she will recover in time."

"Doctor Guillemot all that matters to me is that she is alive. I fell in love and married the person, not the body."

They talked for some time as Doctor explained that Kaya had only been awake for less than two weeks and her mental attitude was only bolstered by having Makar near, but she was as weak as a new born from her experience. Carrying the fetus had taken a toll on her body, then the treatment had added to it, but the future for her was good in that she would recover to be as she once was before becoming pregnant.

Lieutenant Bascalo was waiting for him as he left the doctor's office and escorted him down one level and nearly to the back of the ship till she came to a door, knocked twice on it and opened it for him. Michael stepped through the door and was shocked at what he saw before him.

Michael had help liberate a slaver camp when he was a Cadet Lieutenant and the women that he helped liberate looked in better condition than Kaya did as she sat in a hover chair looking at him. Those women had been physically and sexual abused, but Kaya looked as if she had not survived her treatment.

Kaya was dressed in a simple gown with a blanket on her lap covering her legs and feet. Her head was covered with a scarf and there was no hint of her long, silvery hair to be seen. Her face was drawn, shallow and ashen in color and her arms, uncovered by the sleeves of the gown looked like sticks compared to the muscles she once had.

He walked to her, dropped to his knees at her feet and laid his head in her lap as he began to cry. She spoke to him in a weak voice.

"Michael my love, why are you crying?"

"Look what I have done to you Kaya. Please forgive me for causing this."

"Michael, you are not to blame for this, I am. I softy planted the desire in you to take my body, to use me for your pleasure. I needed you to complete my father's project, and each time we met, I gave you more desire for me. No Michael, this is my fault, not yours, but neither of us considered falling in love. And Michael, you gave me the seed to give you a strong son. Rejoice Michael for my mission to complete, my father's project has ended with success, and in time I will once again be the woman you married in form and shall always be in my heart."

"But the suffering you endured for your project, to give me a child. The pain in my heart is so great I almost wish I was dead to have caused you such misery."

"Enough of this Michael. Come higher and let me taste your kiss on my lips, or is my appearance so hideous that you cannot bring yourself to do that?"

"Oh, saints no Kaya! You will always be beautiful in my eyes."

Michael slowly rose up and leaned in, took her face in his hands and gently kissed her. She put her arms around his neck, but he could tell she did not have the strength to hold him as she once had. When they broke the kiss, he reached up and pulled the scarf from her head to see she was completely bald.

"Oh, Michael why did you do that?"

"Doctor Guillemot said there was side effects to your treatment, but she did not specify what they were."

"Yes, this is one effect of my treatment Michael and they tell me my hair will return in time. But Michael, in curing me they removed my ability to enter your mind. I no longer have psychic ability. I am a normal human now."

"Maybe it will return once you are well?"

"No Michael, it is gone and to be honest, it is a burden that I do not mind losing. Now would you like to see your son?"

"Yes, I would."

Kaya pressed a button on her hover chair and within a minute, the door connecting her room to another opened with one of the female Lancers entering with an infant in her arms. As they came closer to Kaya, Makar began to lean out as if ready to jump into Kaya's awaiting arms. When he was in Kaya's arms he put his arms around her neck and held onto her as if she was going to run away.

"Makar, turn around and look at your father. Come on now, say hello to your father."

Makar turned to look at Michael and gibbered at Michael. Michael held his arms out to Makar.

"Makar, come here, let me give you a hug."

Makar held onto his mother and just looked at his father.

"Michael, give me a kiss, and let Makar know you are important to me."

Michael leaned up and as he gave Kaya a kiss, Makar tried to push them apart. Michael broke the kiss and laughed as he took Makar in hand and lifted him from his mother.

"Makar my son, I think you and I shall have a great amount of fun when you grow older, but if I wish to kiss your mother, I will, and you will just have to get used to it."

Makar scowled at his father then hit Michael on the nose. Michael laughed then with only a finger, bumped Makar on the nose which caused Makar to go wide eyed before hitting Michael again. Michael tapped him again on the nose as he spoke to him.

"Makar, I can do this all day." As he tapped Makar again.

Makar then changed tactics and began to whimper as if he was going to cry.

"Makar, if you hit me, I'll give it back to you so forget crying about getting hit back. Now give your Dada a hug, then I'll give you back to your mother."

Makar looked at his father, then at his mother who was smiling at them. He seemed to know he had lost this battle and leaned in, putting one arm around Michael's neck. Michael kissed him on the cheek which cause Makar to giggle due to Michael's beard. Michael kept his word and handed him back to Kaya.

"He's going to be a handful Kaya."

"Yes, he's already crawling and trying to find his voice. He has the Lancers wrapped around his little finger too."

"How did the two of you bond so fast if you were in a coma?"

"Makar was placed next to me whenever he was not being fed or having his bottom cleaned. I think it is instinct on his part that I am his mother and once I was awake, we have rarely been apart, just him and me. Once we are in my apartment, he will most likely take to you once he gets to know you better."

They talked for over an hour about what the future might hold for them as Makar slowly became friendly with Michael. Kaya told him that she would spend another month on the Jilena as she recovered from her treatment. Michael told her he would visit every chance he could, but there were still things to do on the mountain helping Titus with the search of the cavern complex.

They parted after a long kiss with Makar again trying to separate them before he pulled at Michael's beard. Michael laughed and gave Makar a hug and kiss on the forehead before leaving.

Missing Pieces

Titus summoned Michael to the cavern from the Ranger training camp to consult with him. They stood in the middle of the cavern on a scaffold, so they could get a panoramic view of the cavern.

"Captain Denoyelles, what do you see as you look around the cavern?"

"Commander, are you asking what I see, or do not see? What I do not see is the symmetry of the tunnel lay-out. It's as if there is a tunnel missing right over there." Michael pointed to a blank portion of the cavern wall.

"I agree Captain. We have measured the distance between tunnels and they are exact to within fifty centimeters, but there is that blank place which, if you account for the measurements between tunnels, there is room for another one. Now why isn't there a tunnel? Was the physical structure of the rock formation unstable there so it has been blocked, sealed over, or is there a tunnel that has been sealed to hide something?"

"Very possible either theory is correct. What's your plan Commander?"

"I think a core drill about two meters from the cavern floor on center between the open tunnels on either side. If there is a tunnel hidden behind the material the cavern is sealed with, we should find it, or find nothing but rock."

Titus had one of their mining engineers bring in a ten-centimeter core drill and began the process. Going through the outer layer of sealant was a slow process to prevent burning up the drill. After twenty centimeters, the drill was shifted to another location along the wall as a test hole to check the depth of the sealant. The hole there went seven centimeters until they hit rock.

They moved back to the original hole and began to drill again. A new core drill had to be made to account for the additional depth and after two weeks, they had bored thirty centimeters when they hit what appeared to be metal. It took another two days to get the core plug out of the wall before they could look inside the hole to examine what they had hit.

The Navy was contacted about bringing in a laser torch to cut through the metal obstruction. They first tested the laser on the plug of sealant to insure they would not cause a fire while cutting through the metal obstruction. The material melted, but did not burn.

It took three passes before they could open the hole for a micro-camera could be passed through once it cooled enough. All the camera could see was another tunnel, but one discovery was important in that the metal they had cut through was nearly twice the thickness of the plate sealing the tunnel entrance which they first burned through.

Another test burn of the sealant showed it would not catch fire but as it melted, it resealed, itself where a cutting blade removed the material. Titus order special cutting blades that could reach the expected depth and the saws reconfigured to handle the cutting. Holes were drilled into the sealant to attach the saw frames as they waited for the new blades to arrive.

Michael found himself with too much time on his hands at the cavern and the training site as McKenzie had things under control there. He began returning to Kaya as often as possible and even spent as many nights with here when practical. Kaya had a full-size bed brought in to her compartment, and even though they could only cuddle at night, it eased the pain of separation between them

Makar also joined them in bed and soon came to understand that Michael was part of his family since his mother showed Michael as much love as he received. Michael began to join Makar in his nursery compartment and played with him as they slowly bonded. The one thing Michael never attempted was to enter Makar's mind and plant the feelings of love he had for him. Michael wanted Makar's love to be a genuine as humanly possible.

Jiazi often came to visit her daughter and grandson as they discussed the problems of entering the Federation, and the problems Michael and the Duke had explained to them. Regardless of her physical condition, Kaya was still the Princess of Bellus and ruler of the people. Kaya decided a meeting of the full council was required as soon as possible.

Michael was at the cavern when the notice of the meeting aboard the Jilena came. The vertical cuts through the sealant had been completed and they were roughly halfway through the horizontal at the top of the portal they were cutting. Titus claimed he could not attend since this project required his attention. Michael gave him a lesson in command.

"Commander Titus, how do you justify staying here, watching a blade cut through that sealant when you have been called to a meeting of the Council which you are a valuable member of?"

"Captain Denoyelles, the Council has made this project my responsibility. What kind of commander would I be to leave here for the Capital while my men and women work to complete this project."

"For one Commander, you would be an officer who is responding to a call from those who command you. Second, you have appointed officers and Sergeants and given them the mission of opening that tunnel. Now either you trust them to complete their mission, or you stand back and oversee them as they complete their mission. Which do you think develops trust between yourself and those people?"

Titus stood for a long time thinking about what Michael had just said before responding.

"By my standing here, watching the work, I am giving them the idea that I do not trust them to do the job and complete the mission. Yes, Captain Denoyelles, I can see how that can created a measure of distrust between myself and my people, even if I do have complete faith in them."

Neither man spoke as Michael just smiled knowing that Titus understood the lesson. Titus broke their verbal silence, but not directed to Michael.

"Lieutenant Rohrwacher!" Titus called out.

A female Ranger trotted over to Titus.

"Sir?"

"Lieutenant Rohrwacher, I have been called to the Capital to meet with the Princess and the Council. I leave the opening of the tunnel in your capable hands. Keep up the good work Lieutenant, I'll return once the Council has adjourned which might take a couple days."

"Yes Sir, we'll stay on this, and the Navy is here to advise if we have any problems."

"Carry on Lieutenant."

Rohrwacher saluted Titus and turned back to the job of opening the tunnel. Titus looked at Michael who was smiling.

"I think I did that right, didn't I Captain?"

"You did very well Commander. I hope you noticed how the Lieutenant seemed to straighten up, and glow from the fact you trusted her to handle the mission. That was pride showing on her face, pride in knowing her Commander trusted her to complete the mission on her own. Shall we go meet with the Council?"

The meeting of the Council was held in Kaya's compartment on the Jilena with extra seating brought in and Michael electing to stand behind Kaya instead of sitting. Kaya opened the meeting as per protocol.

"Council of Bellus, I asked you to meet me here today because we have some serious considerations to deal with in reference to the Federation. I have met with Duke Denoyelles twice inquiring his opinion of the problems we, the Bellus people, will bring to the Federation. I have also discussed these things with Prince Michael on several occasions, and although I feel he has

176

given me good advice, he has stated that any decision is mine and the Council's alone, since he claims no right of decision. Do I hear any debate on Prince Michael's position before the Council?"

"Prince Michael, I would ask you a question?"

"Certainly, Lord Ujorn, I will answer any question with honesty as deception or lies have no value."

"We, the Council, have learned that the Denoyelles family is considered the most powerful family within the Federation and the richest. What do you have to gain from us, the people of Bellusarian?"

"Lord Ujorn, I gained a wife and son. Beyond that I have no desire for gains from the people of Bellus. The Duke's father, my great-grandfather, inherited an entire planetary system that eventually made him the wealthiest man in the universe, yet he despised that wealth. But he used that wealth to change the Federation, change the universe as we know it for the betterment of humanity. He then laid that same requirement upon his descendants. We are taught from an early age it is not the wealth of the family that makes us wealthy, but how we use that wealth for the betterment of humanity."

"How does a family become so wealthy while giving so much to the people who need it?" This came from Jiazi.

"Lady Jiazi, the Denoyelles businesses succeed because our employees are the best paid in the Federation. They work hard to insure whichever business they are working at is successful which insures their pay. Several employees have become wealthy in their own right, by developing an idea for a business that the family supports, and becomes a small partner in while allowing that individual to succeed or fail on their own. Other businesses would take those ideas and build the companies themselves, and if the employee was lucky, he might receive a small compensation for his idea."

Michael paused for a moment.

"But we do not give money or goods away to those who need them. Granted there are those who need help and we insure they get that help, but to blindly give to those in need can produce an individual who will always be in need with their hand out for someone else to fill. No, we give and support many projects that help the needy, but the needy also have to show they are trying to help themselves first and foremost."

"Thank you, Prince Michael, but back to my original question. What does the Denoyelles family have to gain from helping we Bellusarians?" Lord Ujorn once more asked.

"My Grandfather, the Duke stood before the Federation Congress and vowed that we, the Denoyelles, have no financial gain in mind by helping the Bellusarians. Before I contacted the Duke, I envisioned a people needing help to move from their seclusion into the universe. If you are not aware of it, this very ship was given to the purpose of helping humanity and more directly the Bellusarian people with the problems plaguing the ability to conceive and produce the next generation. The Captain and crew are paid from Denoyelles funds with the mission of supporting the needs of the Doctors and scientists of Altair. What the Denoyelles family has received in return is the most precious of gifts, my son Makar. And if my wife, the Princess Kaya wishes another child, she will be able to conceive and carry to term as a normal human mother."

"Thank you, Prince Michael for your honesty and the explanation of your lineage." Commented Lord Ujorn.

Kaya then moved the meeting to the perceived threats to Federation security from the technology of the Bellusarians. The Capital and the half dozen small communities that had been concealed with the cloaking devices no longer needed such protection, and the individual devices used only by the Foresters to observe the animal population could be done away with.

The debate on those devices went for nearly an hour before Michael once again spoke up.

"Council, you must consider the effects of trade with other planets in this matter. The economic system in which you have been raised in is an idyllic system which has been sought after by others over the eons, but has never worked until your people were taught it. But it has never been faced with one factor of life that can destroy what you have. That is greed."

Michael watched the faces of the Council members as he paused.

"Your markets are open and if someone needs something they receive it. Everyone produces to support the population without regard of cost since the cost is spread out to everyone equally. The miners who struggle to remove the metals needed are in turn repaid with food, clothing and a place to shelter. I can go on for hours, but I think each of you understand your system much better than I do."

Michael could not help but see the nods of agreement from the Council.

"But once trade is introduced, once off-worlders introduce Crowns for produce, then the term wealth and greed will become known to all. Everyone will learn that their labors have value beyond what they have been raised to know. Then when items produced off world are introduced to the Bellus people that comes with a price, how do you insure those items are given equally to the people? You cannot. All it takes is one person to have a desire for something offered, but cannot afford, to sell a cloaking device for less than what it is really worth. Desire begets greed when the prospect of having something no others have. This is the greatest fear my family has for Bellus."

Kaya spoke before any of the Council could.

"Honored Council, husband or not, Prince Michael makes a valid case for the destruction of our cloaking technology. If it falls into the wrong hands it can bring destruction to the Federation and ultimately Bellus. I put it to you to vote to destroy that which can ultimately destroy us. Council, what say you?"

One by one the Council voted to destroy the cloaking technology with additional questions being asked of Michael before some members voted. Titus advised the Council that the Foresters had a solid accounting of who had the devices and those in storage, plus the ones that were located to hide the communities.

Once the vote was confirmed, Titus was given the responsibility of having his Rangers collect and account for every device before destroying them. Michael was asked to oversee, to witness the destruction of the devices. He recommended that his Lieutenant McKenzie be the observer to insure destruction without telling him exactly what they were destroying. If the count was correct before and after destruction, then all that matters is a member of the Fleet has witnessed it. This would also remove a Denoyelles from taking part in said destruction. His suggestion was accepted.

Titus gave the orders to first gather the devices concealing the communities along with the technology to build more. Any item that was involved in producing the devices were to be removed and taken to a site near the Ranger training camp for destruction. Titus followed Michael's earlier suggestion concerning trusting a subordinate to deal with the task.

Michael spent the night with Kaya and Makar before returning to the cavern as word had come to them the sealant had been cut through, and work was progressing on cutting through the metal door. They had talked for several hours about the loss of her psychic powers and the possibility that this would occur to everyone that the Altairians treated to cure their birthing problems.

Kaya understood the Duke's concern about the Bellusarian people entering the Federation with the ability to read minds and even control them. She told Michael having the ability was a great burden on her and she was relieved to have it removed from her.

When Michael returned to the cavern, he found that the opening to the tunnel was nearly completed. Titus was suited up for a fight with his carbine hanging in front and he had a squad behind him ready for action. When the last laser cut was made, four Rangers struck it with a heavy ram causing it to fall back, making a loud ringing sound as it struck the floor.

Two large lights were already prepared and the first two Rangers through the door pulled them in, and set them so the beams of light would travel down the tunnel. Titus was the next individual into the tunnel along with his squad. Down the tunnel they went with a single person stopping in front of each door they found to watch it until more lightening could be brought it.

Titus stopped at the edge of available light with the last four of his squad and positioned them to watch the darkness. As he moved back up the tunnel he checked each door finding them all secured. Lights were being brought in with the scaffolding to light the tunnel as others rigged a manner to pull the remains of the access away from inside the tunnel.

Lighting the tunnel went quick as they had plenty of practice doing the other tunnels, plus the equipment was already laid out ahead of time. As the engineers moved down the tunnel, additional Rangers entered and prepped the doors with explosives, then just stood back waiting and watching.

Titus ordered all fuses to be connected and as the engineers finished up the lighting and moved back out of the tunnel, the Rangers backed out connecting the fuses, so they would all blow at once. When Lieutenant Rohrwacher advised Titus that the charges were ready, he smiled and told her to blow the doors. She smiled as she saluted and gave the orders to clear everyone from in front of the tunnel entrance as she moved to the detonator.

Rohrwacher looked around to insure no one was in the possible line of flight of debris then called out a warning before removing the safety cap from the detonator. She called out a second warning, then pressed the detonator button on the firing panel. There was a slight rippling effect of the explosives moving down the tunnel then silence. Rohrwacher watched the seconds move by on her wrist chronometer and at sixty seconds gave the command to move the ventilation fans into the tunnel entrance.

As the fans were being put in place, Rohrwacher ordered four Rangers to watch the tunnel as the dust and smoke cleared. The fans blew across the floor then up and out the top of the tunnel opening. Other fans were placed to blow the exhaust from the tunnel out into the cavern. No one made an attempt to enter the tunnel for nearly an hour as it cleared.

When Titus started to move to the tunnel, Rohrwacher stepped in front of him and began to give orders moving people into the tunnel. She never spoke to Titus and Michael almost laughed at the look on Titus' face as Rohrwacher took command of the situation.

Rohrwacher moved her people from door to door opening each and using hand spotlights to see what was inside each room. At the fifth door, she stepped back out and commanded everyone to hold in place as she waved Titus forward. Michael could feel the tension coming from Rohrwacher as he moved up with Titus.

"Commander, I'm not sure what we have in there, but it feels wrong."

Titus looked at Michael before he moved to the entrance to the room. Michael took a hand-held light from a Ranger then stepped inside the room past Titus. He only took a step before he pulled the katana from its sheath on his back. The room was filled with tables lined in order and four across the width of the room. On each table was what appeared to be a body covered in white cloth. There was no odor in the room other than the smell of the explosives which opened it.

Michael reached out to find life in this room, but he detected no life, only death.

"Michael are you alright?" It was Titus's voice from behind him.

"Yeah Titus, I'm alright. We need to get this room lighted as quick as possible and a doctor in here. We are also going to need body bags, a lot of them."

As he turned back to the door another thing crossed his mind.

"No one enters without biological protection. Everyone who has entered needs to be isolated until the doctors can insure we have not been infected with something that might kill us. Let's get out of here and seal the door for now."

Titus began giving orders and the entrance to the tunnel was sealed with a heavy tarp until a doctor could be brought down from one of the ships in orbit. An isolation tent was erected in front of the tunnel entrance for the doctors to use as they checked each individual what had been in the tunnel.

The examines were quick as blood was checked along with scans of the lungs to insure they had not breathed in any contaminates. Their clothing was scanned and give a clean bill before each person was sent out to join their friends in the cavern.

As that was happening, the engineers had covered themselves against chemical and biological contaminates then entered the tunnel with the equipment to light the room with the bodies. They hung the first lights and two spot lights before backing out of the room and waiting for further orders.

Titus order that no one entered the tunnel without protective gear, and one by one the Rangers entered prepared for opening the rest of the rooms.

The doctors entered the room with the bodies and began to exam the first ones with Titus and Michael observing. The first bodies were human in form, both male and females laid out as if being prepared for autopsy. There were no tags or charts to tell who these people were as a detail of Rangers were brought in with body bags and carefully placed each cadaver in a bag marking each bag with a table numbering scheme that Michael suggested.

About halfway down the room the bodies began to change until they appeared to be Centaurians, but some of their appearance told Michael they were not Centaurians. Michael told Titus that he believed that those bodies were of the Masters, but only DNA tests would tell them the truth.

Once back into the cavern, the doctors put all the data taken with hand held devices into their field computer and the results were confusing. All of the bodies belonged to the same race of humanoid people. Only minor differences in DNA was present which may account for the fur covering of their bodies.

Michael suggested the bodies be turned over to the Altairians for a complete genetic exam before final disposition of their bodies could be arranged. Titus agreed, and a heavy transport was arranged to take the bodies to the Jilena to be examined.

No more bodies were found as the rooms were opened, but one room had what appeared to be a computer system. As before no power supplies could be found and nothing they did could power the system as with the other pieces of equipment.

One of the engineers noted that the mechanical monsters used Q-wave power sources and after some experimenting he rigged several together and hooked them to a ground vehicle in the cavern. It partially powered up the control panel with one of the Rangers advising that if the language was close enough one of the readings was low power. Several more power sources were brought it and soon the vehicle came up to full power.

Once that was figured out the Q-wave power sources were dismantled and taken back out of the cavern. The Navy Chief told Michael the reason the Fleet did not use Q-wave as a power source was long term exposure caused damage to the human body including sterility in men. Titus looked at Michael as if he had just discovered the pleasures of sex.

"Michael all of our equipment, devices here use Q-wave as was taught to our ancestors by the Masters. Could this be the cause of our medical problems?"

"Commander, I have no idea, but I think this is something we need to advise the Altairians about."

Heritage

Kaya stayed aboard the Jilena two weeks longer than predicted as she gained weight and was given physical therapy to regain muscle she had lost while in her coma.

When she moved into her apartment in the Cathedral, she had a crib brought in and made Makar sleep in it instead of in bed with her. Makar protested as any infant would, but his grandmother Jiazi gave him a stuffed bera made from the actual fur of the creature and Makar pulled it close as he laid down and went to sleep.

Michael spent as much time as he could with Kaya and Makar, but insisted that Kaya improve more before they engaged in any manner of pleasure.

It was over a month after Kaya returned to her apartment that Michael arrived to find that Makar was spending the night with his grandmother and Kaya was ready to once more take Michael to bed. They found that even without the psychic link they once had their passion in bed was as pleasant as ever.

The Altairians were slowly examining the bodies taken from the cavern building a DNA profile on each body and the group. But from what they had discovered up to that point was that they all came from the same gene pool.

Doctor Guillemot called for a meeting with Michael alone which bothered him since Kaya was returning each day for therapy and keeping a check on her improving health. He sat in her office afraid that something was wrong with Kaya.

"Baron Denoyelles, I asked you to come alone because what we have discovered about the bodies found in the mountains. We have conducted every test known, and ran most twice to insure no mistakes. But we are puzzled about the good condition of the bodies we have in our labs. As you know I sent a team to the cavern to examine the room they were found in and nothing was found to indication a measure of preservation. This is puzzling."

"Yes, Doctor, I also noticed that situation."

"Anyway, putting that aside, we have compared the DNA of the bodies against the DNA of Princess Kaya. After doing that we asked for samples of other members of the Bellusarian race for further comparison. Unless we have made a serious mistake, which I do not believe we have made, the Bellusarian race are the remains of the Masters. They are not separate, but one and the same."

"Doctor Guillemot that does not make sense. The Masters travel through the universe long before humans on Earth took to the skies in canvas aircraft. There is nothing here on Bellus to even allow these people to even enter an orbit much less travel to another planet and the people here are without the fur of the Masters."

"The lack of fur can be explained through genetic manipulation during the search for a cure to their problems. Now let in introduce a theory to you."

"Sure, go ahead." Michael responded.

"We feel that once the last settlement of the Masters is discovered and their space craft examined, it will be found they used Q-wave as their primary power source which actually lead to their demise. The people they left behind were the results of their genetic experiments and were left behind because they would not fit into the society of the Masters at their home planet. Their history of being left behind because they were from Earth was planted in their history to protect them from the truth, and since they had contact with small doses of the Q-wave radiation, it took them longer to suffer the consequences than the space travelers. After eons of telling your descendants a story it becomes myth or legend."

"Alright Doctor. What do we do now?"

"Baron Denoyelles, or should I address you as Prince Michael. The choice is yours. We Altairians will never expose the truth without official disclosure prior to that event."

Michael sat and thought about the effects this could have on the Bellusarians and could not find a good answer to the problem that was just laid in his lap.

186

"Doctor Guillemot is there a cure to the problem they are facing with their population? I mean other than the long process that Kaya was put through?"

"Yes, we have developed a sort of vaccine which in the lab removes the Masters DNA and replaces it with human normal DNA. If predictions are correct they will suffer a few days of illness but will recover and soon their population will once more begin to grow."

"What of the effects of Q-wave radiation?"

"This is something that you will have to take to the Council and find a new method of supplying power to the people. Even with the vaccine, if they continue to use Q-wave as a power source, in a few generations the problem will return."

"Doctor, I think we shall keep the knowledge of the heritage of the Bellusarian people as they believe it already is. There is nothing to be gained to destroy the image they have of themselves."

Michael knew the next step was to convince the Council to ask for help in finding a new power source, then to have the people vaccinated. He wasn't sure how he could do this, but he had no choice but to try.

"Doctor one last thing. Is the vaccine ready for human trials?"

"Yes Baron, it is. We just have to locate some volunteers as test subjects."

"You have your first sitting in front of you. I'm part Centaurian as you already know. The Council is aware of my genetic profile so if I can approach them with the results of the vaccine on myself, then it will make my path to convince them to submit much easier."

Deep inside Michael only wanted the psychic ability gone and return to a normal life as it was wearing on him.

"Certainly Baron, when would you like to take the vaccine?"

"Today if possible. I just had a thought, when will Makar be old enough to take the vaccine?"

"Baron, Makar has already been vaccinated. We did research on his DNA while he was still a fetus and determined he had the same markers as the Princess. Once we knew that our treatment on the Princess was going to be successful, we developed the vaccine and fed it to him through his feeding tube while he was still in the artificial womb."

"Alright then, that explains a few things about him I have been wondering about. So, let's do this Doctor."

Doctor Guillemot took Michael to a lab where the Altairians drew blood for a comparison before giving him the vaccine. He left with a list of symptoms to watch for and returned to the Ranger Training camp to talk to McKenzie about the destruction of the cloaking devices.

McKenzie had an idea for destruction that Michael had to laugh at. Not that it was silly but because it was near genius. Because of the Q-wave power sources if they burned the devices the smoke would spread the particle radiation same as if the blew them up. But the Fleet had remote controlled supply drones for supplying Marines on a planet where a manned vehicle would be at risk of being shot down. McKenzie had worked out the math on the volume and weight of the devices and figured two drones, launched into the systems sun would destroy everything with zero risk to the planet of the people involved.

The other thing McKenzie had worked out was the period of exposure time transporting the devices and loading them into a drone was insufficient to cause medical problems to the personal handling them.

Michael contacted the Rostislav and made the arrangements. The Rostislav launched two assault boats for the task of lifting the devices into orbit. Two drones were waiting in the hanger bay when the boats returned along with McKenzie in the boat assigned to the training camp. McKenzie closely monitored the movement from the boats to the drones insuring no one kept a souvenir.

188

The last thing to be loaded were three memory cubes that McKenzie had in a kit bag. Once those were in the second drone and sealed he observed both drones loaded into their launch tubes. The Rostislav had left orbit after he had arrived, and moved within range of the drones in reference to the systems sun.

Once he confirmed the launch from the hanger deck, McKenzie went up to the bridge and watched as the drones flew into the sun. The impact of the drones was barely noticed on the screens as they burned up in the sun's corona. No one asked what was contained within the drones as they returned to orbit, and McKenzie returned to the surface.

McKenzie turned over the targeting data to Michael confirming that the mission to destroy all the cloaking devices and information had been completed. He then asked Michael the question he never asked when given the assignment.

"Captain, you and I have served together in some nasty places, so I never questioned your orders to destroy that equipment. But we could have rendered it inoperable by simply removing the power sources. Why was it so important to completely destroy the devices themselves?"

"Mac, I know you have seen the Rangers wearing the individual devices, didn't you ever think to ask what they were?"

"Captain, I figured they were communications devices."

"Yes, they were, but that was not their primary purpose. How would you like to land in a hot zone to find the other side were invisible to you, even if they were close enough to put a bayonet into you?"

"Holy Mother of all Saints! Are you kidding me Captain?"

"No Mac, I'm not. Kaya watched me a long time before she ever exposed herself. Those devices even fool our sensor packs. I'm still confused how Kaya entered my shuttle without setting off the security alarms, but she entered several times while I was asleep and messed with my gear making it seem the planet was haunted."

"Captain I would hate to think what would happen if the slavers got their hands on one of them. Are you sure we got them all?"

"Commander Titus says we had everyone produced in our possession. You had the list so unless the Commander has lied to us, you just destroyed all of them and the memory cubes contained the instructions on manufacturing them. The manufacturing facilities are being dismantled as we speak. No one, and I mean no one knows about their cloaking devices outside the Bellusarians except for the Duke, my father, myself and now you."

"Captain, no one will ever hear of it from me."

Michael left the training camp to return to Kaya at her apartment. He told her what he had done in taking the vaccine. Kaya was upset that he had taken it without talking to her first, but he told her that there would always be decisions both of them would have to make without talking to the other. Michael was already feeling the effect of the vaccine and he went to their bed before he was too weak to do it on his own.

A Bold Plan

Michael spent four days in bed as he suffered from the shakes and sweats as his DNA was altered to human norm. Doctor Guillemot checked on him daily as he progressed through the conversion. On the fifth day, Doctor Guillemot reported that all traces of the Masters DNA had been removed and he should be back to normal in a few days.

Two weeks later, Kaya called for another Council meeting about the Jilena. Michael stood before the Council with examples of his converted DNA to show that it was possible to fix the defects that were slowly killing their race. Doctor Guillemot explained the process and the fact that the Q-wave radiation had mutated the Masters genes. She compared the Bellusarian DNA to Centaurian DNA to show the difference in that the Centaurians had never been subjected to long term exposure to Q-wave radiation.

The Council agreed to call for a meeting of the people of Bellus to advise them of the situation and to plan for each to receive the vaccine in groups so there would be healthy people to care for the ones becoming sick during the conversion.

After Doctor Guillemot left the meeting, Michael then told the Council of the effect the vaccine had on psychic abilities. Both he and Kaya had lost that ability due to the fact it was tied to the Masters DNA. The debate went on for over an hour, but in the end, all Council members agreed that having the ability to read another's mind was a burden. They all voted to take it to the citizens without holding back any information concerning the final results of the treatment.

The meeting hall was packed with Rangers and Foresters standing along the back of the great hall. Michael was surprised to learn that every citizen of Bellus was in the hall for this meeting not knowing how close the race was to extinction.

The Council was formed at the long table on the stage when Kaya in her royal outfit with Michael in his formal Marine dress uniform took the stage with Kaya holding Makar in a jumpsuit made from the same material his mother's clothing was cut from. They took center stage with Michael slightly to the rear of Kaya on her right. When Kaya introduced Makar to the citizens the applause was deafening until Jiazi rapped on the table to quiet the audience.

Kaya told the citizens about her experience and the cause of her near-death due to the mutation of the DNA within her body. She told of the treatment she received from the Altairians which not only saved her life and the life of Makar, but changed her in ways she had never envisioned. Kaya held nothing back as she told of her loss of her psychic abilities, and the peace in which she lived now not having those abilities.

Michael stepped forward and explained how he also had the Masters DNA from his Centaurian grandmother and gave a brief history of the Centaurians for the citizens who were not aware of them. He also admitted to having psychic abilities which were opened to him having met Kaya. Michael then told that he had taken the vaccine offered by the Altairians and the results of that vaccine.

The citizens were given every bit of information possible to allow them to make an informed decision. Kaya held nothing back as she explained that the only hope for their race, for the people of Bellus was to sacrifice the burden of their psychic ability for the ability to procreate and once more grow into a viable population. The Q-wave energy sources were also noted in her dialogue as being dangerous even in the small units they had available to them.

Michael once again entered the discussion by explaining that there were other energy sources available which were much safer in both use, and to the humans utilizing them. He advised them that Duke Denoyelles, his grandfather, was currently arranging for the replacement of the Q-wave sources with safe sources, and would even provide technicians to assist in connecting the new sources to their devices while removing the old ones for disposal.

Once Kaya finished with her part of the meeting, the floor was opened for questions or comments from the citizens. Michael had to smile at how well this took place with everyone patiently waiting their turn to ask a question or make a comment. No bickering or verbal challenging another's view point. One question was directed at Michael.

"Prince Michael, we have heard many things about you and your family. I for one would like to thank you for what you are doing for Bellus, but who, or how can we pay for all those new power sources? We do not use money for transacting deals between one another."

"Citizen, I have discussed this with the Duke. There is an organization on Hanover which his father formed decades ago to help those in need. The Hanover Foundation will obtain the power supplies, and provide the technicians to convert existing power supplies to the newer, safer forms at no cost to Bellus, except for maybe a meal or two. I hope this answers your question."

Kaya was asked by several people what it was like to live without her psychic ability, to which she said at first it seemed unnatural, but after several weeks she said it was peaceful not to have the underlying current of other people's thoughts touching against her mind.

When Makar became fussy, Michael took him off stage and changed his diaper, and fed him while Kaya continued in her responsibility as the Throne of Bellus. It was over three hours before Kaya left the stage, so the Council and the citizens could determine the path of the planet.

There was a question concerning the loss of intelligence from taking the vaccine and removing the psychic abilities. This had been anticipated and a video link to the Jilena and Doctor Guillemot was established after the citizens were once again cautioned about allowing an off-worlder know about those abilities. Doctor answered several questions before the link was broken and the debate went on.

The citizens of Bellus had long agreed that a simple majority was all that was required to pass or make an agreement in the hall but today, the Council asked that they accept a two-thirds majority due to the seriousness of the subject matter. Regardless of how the vote turned out, the majority would rule and those voting against understood they had to abide by the majority. Before the vote was taken, Titus stood and made a simple statement in that if the vote is against taking the vaccine as the whole of the population, then it should be up to the individual to take it on their own. He then stated he would take the vaccine regardless of the vote, and hoped that the lady he was going to ask to be his bond mate would also take it, so they could safely conceive a child.

The Bellusarians had developed a near perfect manner of voting without using ballots or computers. When it came time to vote, those voting no left the hall and were counted as they left. The Council had a solid count of the population and it was simple to subtract those voting no from yes. The population voted over ninety-three percent for the vaccine. Kaya later told Michael that some citizens voted no just to ensure that those unsure of themselves would have others to be with at the end of the vote. But regardless even those who voted no would stand in line for the vaccine out of respect for the rule of the vote.

Once the vote was confirmed, those who had left, reentered the hall to be there as the details were worked out. The Jilena could handle one hundred patients, and this would free up those who would have to care for those vaccinated from having to take away from their labors.

Again, the Council had prepared for the selection process by holding a lottery. A large drum was set up containing the exact amount of numbers as there were citizens. As the people filed out of the hall, they took a disk from the drum, then took it to two Rangers that marked their number by their names. The first one hundred citizens would report to the Jilena the next day for treatment.

Over the next three months, Kaya would go visit those on Jilena who were being treated, and often took Makar along which cheered up those suffering the conversion. By the time the last citizen had been converted, it was reported females were becoming pregnant with their bond mates.

The Final Step

When the last Bellusarian left the Jilena after the conversion, Kaya stood before the Council in the great hall and declared her father's project complete. She then abdicated the throne in favor of an elected Council to rule over the planet. This met with protests from not only the Council, but the citizens. Kaya only bowed to the will of the people once she made it clear that she would sit on the throne only for ceremonial purposes, but she would abstain from any part of governing the planet. This was accepted and written into the laws of Bellus.

By the time the third group of Rangers had completed their basic training, McKenzie and his Marines had taken Bellusarian wives. The Council passed a special edict making them citizens of Bellus with all of them being promoted into the officer ranks of the Rangers. McKenzie was now a Major and mated to Elipida who was promoted to Senior Lieutenant as the administrative officer of the training camp.

Once all of the Rangers had been trained, the camp turned to advance training for officers and Sergeants. The carven in the mountains was cleared of all debris and equipment, then turned into a training site teaching the Rangers on blowing doors and clearing rooms such as the Marines did aboard ships.

With over two hundred fully trained Rangers on the planet's surface, the Fleet pulled all but two ships back from quarantine duty to patrol duty. The Marines aboard the ships left in orbit would often come to the surface for training and live fire exercises. When they engaged in war games, the Marines had nothing but praise for the Rangers.

Once the planet was converted from Q-wave power, the Hanover engineers turned to the vehicles that were found in the cavern. Four of the vehicles were discovered to be high speed, sub-orbital craft which the Rangers took possession of giving them the capability of moving a section of Rangers, not including the pilot and co-pilot, anywhere on the planet in half the time their old craft could move them.

One craft was carefully taken apart then reassembled with each part blue printed for future craft to be built. This also helped identify some of the odds and ends found in the tunnels as repair parts.

Makar was a year old when the Duke sat down with the Council to determine the path towards membership within the Federation. Michael was called in to sit in on the discussions, but Kaya was not which Michael could not understand at the time. It was not until the Duke advised the Council that he could no longer represent the planet at this stage of negotiations that Michael's part in this became clear.

Only a citizen of the planet could represent them before the Federation. An ambassador to act for the good of Bellus before Congress and the Federation Council. Michael reminded his grandfather that he was a serving Federation Marine officer and born on Denoyelles. The Duke then reminded Michael that he was married to the throne of Bellus, and the Prince of Bellus even if it was only a ceremonial title and position. Jiazi commented that even though it is not stated in their laws, Michael's being married to a Bellusarian gave him citizenship to Bellus.

The Duke drove the nail into the debate when he plainly stated who was the most qualified to stand before the Federation than Michael was? As well as the Council ruled the planet, they had no experience in dealing with off-worlders where as Michael was raised amongst those same people, and had to interact with them as a Marine. Michael's knowledge of the Federation would play in the favor of Bellus.

Michael felt trapped, but knew his grandfather was looking out for not only him, but the Bellusarian people. It would require Michael to tender his resignation to the Marines, but he could finally settle down and raise a family with Kaya. This thought also brought up the fact he would be gone for months at a time, away from Kaya. Jiazi smiled when she told him that Kaya would go with him and he could raise his family on Hanover as well as she could on Bellus.

When Michael returned to their apartment and told Kaya of the decision of the Council, she only smiled and asked when they would be leaving for Hanover.

That evening the Duke and Duchess had dinner with Michael and Kaya in the Royal apartment. Makar had never met Ireesha, his great-grandmother and was taken by the soft fur on her face. As Ireesha entertained Makar, the Duke produced a satchel containing documents which Michael needed to sign. At first Michael thought it was the documents to make him the Ambassador, but they were the documents Michael had to sign to take control of his inheritance.

Kaya had trouble understanding wealth especially the kind that the Denoyelles family had control of as she listened to the Duke explain each document before Michael signed acceptance for that transaction.

She did somewhat understand the Michael owned property in and around the Hanover capital, which meant they had a place to live and raise a family. Michael selected a manor house sitting on twenty hectares inside Hanover as the future Embassy of Bellus. It was a walled compound with plenty of ground to build a guard barracks and expand the manor as needed to fit the needs of the Embassy.

Michael read the federation guidelines for the establishment of an Embassy, then contacted Titus to come to the apartment. He asked Titus to select a Ranger section to go to Hanover as the Embassy Security Detail. The Duke told Titus that he would take the section to Hanover when he left in three days, so they could receive special training on security from the Lancers.

When Titus asked who the Lancers were, both the Duke and Michael smiled and turned to Ireesha for her to answer. Titus left shaking his head with the knowledge that Makar's great-grandmother had once been a mercenary, a soldier who fought for money.

Michael then went to the Council and asked for five people to work in the Embassy as his assistants. The Duke would arrange for them to be trained in protocol and other activities they would have to deal with on a daily basis. All that was left was to arrange transportation to Hanover since Bellus did not have a single interstellar capable vehicle.

Three weeks after the Duke left for Hanover, a Presidential Class space yacht entered orbit over Bellus and requested permission to land. When Bellus Control asked the purpose for landing, the response required Control to contact Michael. The ship was listed as the personal space yacht of the Baron Denoyelles and was there to take him to Hanover at his pleasure.

Michael laughed when he discovered the Captain of his personal yacht was also the son of his aunt, his father's sister who had retired from the Fleet. The ship was newly commissioned and the flight to Bellus from Denoyelles was its shake-down cruise. The yacht had not been given a name, so Michael had it christened Bellus One.

Two weeks later Michael, Kaya, and Makar boarded the Bellus One with his small staff for Hanover. They also found six Lancers under the employment of the Duke on board to provide security until the Bellusarians finished their training on Hanover.

The landing on Hanover was met by Federation officials who welcomed the Ambassador of Bellus to Hanover along with the Royal Princess and young Prince. Michael almost found it comical since he had known some of the officials for years before becoming a Marine, but the process was a formal setting designed to recognize Michael's new status within the Federation.

When Michael addressed the Federation Congress, his grandfather was in the audience representing Hanover and his father representing Denoyelles. He submitted his credentials to the Congress and the application for Bellus to join the Federation.

During his short speech before Congress, Michael offered Bellus as port of call, and land for a Fleet Support Facility on the edge of unknown, uncharted space. He asked for nothing in return except peace.

Bellus was accepted within the Federation on the first roll-call vote. Michael declared his manor within the city of Hanover as property of Bellus, and the Embassy of Bellus.

Within days his desk in the Embassy was covered with trade agreements from all over the Federation. His concern that he was not up to the task dealing in business was eased when the Duke quietly sent his best broker to assist Michael, to ensure that no one would be able to take advantage of Michael's inexperience.

The Closing Act

Michael was the Bellusarian Ambassador to the Federation for thirty-five years. Kaya gave him two daughters, Sayoko and Violante after Makar then another son, Crispen before she told him their family was large enough.

Makar went to the university on Hanover when he wasn't living in the mud with the Lancers learning skills he never would have learned on Bellus. Kaya insured he spent as much time on Bellus as possible, and even took him into the wilds as she once did, and taught him about the animals and foods available if you knew where to look.

When he graduated from the university, he returned to Bellus and joined the Rangers as common soldier. Bellus prospered and had ships built on Denoyelles for trade and travel. Makar rose to the rank of Senior Lieutenant when he was posted as the senior officer aboard a Bellusarian Heavy Destroyer which went deep into uncharted space to explorer, and chart the planets yet discovered.

He was wounded in a skirmish with slavers during his second year, but held his ground as his men rallied on him to defeat the slavers. They relieved a slavers camp before he allowed himself to be evacuated for treatment of his wounds.

Makar returned to Bellus with a two-rank promotion and took over the Ranger Training School as its commander. It was here he met then married the second daughter of McKenzie and Elpidia, who gave him three sons. He would retire on Bellus years later as Commandant of Rangers. In time, Makar would become the Duke Denoyelles as would his eldest son.

Sayoko entered medicine out of the university, studying on Altair before becoming a ship's surgeon in the Fleet. After the Fleet, she settled on Bellus where she married Titus's eldest son.

Violante fell in love with Bellus during one of the many trips she took there with her mother. She finished her university, then went to Bellus where she joined the new Foresters. She married another Forester her second year on Bellus and had five children between her trips into the wild surveying the animal life. She retired as a Captain of Foresters.

Crispen followed his father into the Marines. As a Lieutenant, he showed such fearlessness in combat, that his commanding officer prohibited him from hazardous assignments out of fear he would be killed. He was assigned to the Fleet Base on Bellus as the Executive Officer of the Base Security Detachment until his enlistment was up. He stayed on Bellus, joining the Rangers and served under his brother Makar as the Ranger Operations Officer until both retired.

Crispen married an Altairian doctor stationed on Bellus and had two children.

Michael and Kaya returned to Bellus as often as they could, building a home at the foot of the Southern Mountains for when they visited and later retired. Even after Michael became the Duke Denoyelles, he only left Bellus when the family business demanded it. Michael and Kaya lived their lives surrounded by their grandchildren then later great-grandchildren.

Fate drew Michael and Kaya together into a lifetime of love for each other. They were buried side by side at the foot of the mountains that one was raised to fear, and the other was drawn too because of a myth.

Kaya wrote in her book, The Bellus Project, that she had hoped a child between her and Michael would give them a way to cure the problems of her people. But what it did was open the door so people who could really help, passed through and not only cured the disease which was destroying the Bellusarian race, but gave them the Universe to explore.

About The Author

Leon Michaels is the author of several novels and short stories that reflect his twenty-three years of military service. Michaels enlisted in the Marine Corps in 1970 and has memberships in the Veterans of Foreign Wars, the American Legion, the Disabled American Veterans organizations, NRA, and Rotary International. In 1971, he married his high school sweetheart, raised three daughters and has three grandsons. He calls Creek County, Oklahoma home.

Made in the USA
Columbia, SC
18 August 2018